Bittersweet Sixteen

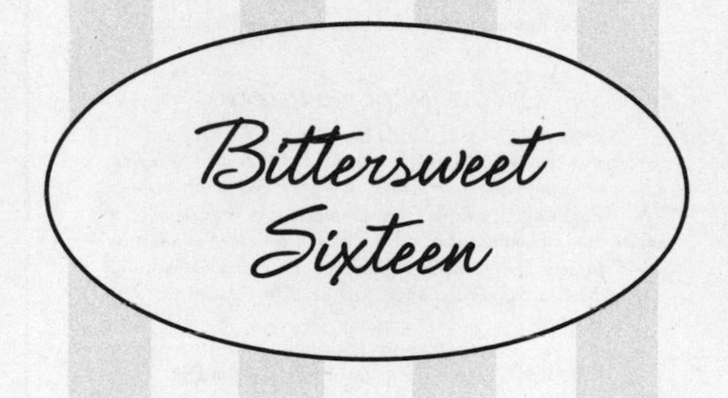

CARRIE KARASYOV & JILL KARGMAN

HarperTeen is an imprint of HarperCollins Publishers.

Bittersweet Sixteen

 For information address HarperCollins Children's Books, a division of HarperCollins Publishers, 1350 Avenue of the Americas, New York, NY 10019.

www.harperteen.com

Library of Congress Cataloging-in-Publication Data
Karasyov, Carrie.
Kargman, Jill.
Bittersweet sixteen / Carrie Karasyov and Jill Kargman.—1st ed.
p. cm.
Summary: A student at New York's most exclusive preparatory school for girls deals with the mayhem of "Sweet Sixteen" birthday parties given by the ultra-wealthy.
ISBN-13: 978-0-06-077846-0 — ISBN-10: 0-06-077846-6
[1. Preparatory schools—Fiction. 2. High schools—Fiction. 3. Schools—Fiction. 4. Friendship—Fiction. 5. Birthdays—Fiction. 6. Parties—Fiction. 7. New York (N.Y.)—Fiction.] I. Kargman, Jill. II. Title.
PZ7.K1344Bit 2006 2005017975
[Fic]—dc22

Typography by Sasha Illingworth

❖

First paperback edition, 2007

Carrie & Jill thank . . .

. . . the awesome HarperCollins posse of Tara Weikum for all the great guidance, and also Alix Reid for the chance to write this book. The ICM ladies: Amanda Urban, Jennifer Joel, and the left coasters Stacey Rosenfelt and Josie Freedman, plus our lawyers Steven Beer and Mary Miles.

Carrie thanks . . . my family, friends, and minor acquaintances, with a particular shout-out to Vas, James, Peter, and the Huitzes (Lesbia, Emilio, Bryan, Jairo, Emily, and Juana).

Jill thanks . . . my amazing fam: Major bow-down worshipful thanks to Mom, Dad, and Will, who kept me grounded through all the bumpy teen-angsty dramas, Ruth Kopelman, Herzl Franco, the Kargs, espesh Bess & Soph, who keep me up on the Lolita lingo ("ridonculous is the new ridiculous"). And to the chère posse I've known over half my life: Dana Jones, Trip Cullman, Lisa Turvey & Lauren Duff, who saved high school from heinosity, and to Jeannie Stern and Vanessa Eastman, my sistas who I feel I've known and loved just as long. And to Harry and Sadie for being the light at the end of the growing-up tunnel.

Chapter One

There's one thing you have to know. In the world of private schools, penthouses on Park Avenue, chauffeur-driven Bentleys, and $100-a-plate family dinners at Le Cirque, one thing reigns supreme as the pinnacle of a tenth-grade girl's social calendar in New York: the almighty Sweet Sixteen birthday extravaganza.

It was the first day of school, sophomore year. That September anticipatory stress was coursing through every capillary of every student, and *not* because of the backbreaking textbooks already tucked into our Marc Jacobs bags for the nightly grind. It was because the competition for the best Sweet Sixteen soiree was about to start, and it was steep. I mean, *way* more cutthroat than the honor society plaque.

Let me back up. My name is Laura Finnegan and I live in New York City. My school is not your average football 'n' cheerleader, pom-pom, pep-rally, flag-waving, all-American Rydell High kind of place. No varsity letters, no football games, no prom king . . . no prom. See, my school, Tate Academy, is—gasp—*all girls*. I know, nightmare, right? Oh, and did I mention the uniform? Gray pleated skirt and white button-down shirt. Not that we really care; I mean, who are we trying to flirt with by our lockers? No one! Oh, and btw, we don't even *have* lockers; we have carpeted lounges with individual closets opening onto the couch-filled room.

See, Tate is the top private all-girls academy in New York, a bastion of education and refinement that has been enlightening the city's finest young ladies for over two hundred years. Jackie O. personally saw to its landmark preservation in the eighties, when the ivy was eating away at the historic limestone facade. Located on the überposh Upper East Side, it boasts a student directory where most of the last names are the same as *Fortune* 500 companies.

Except for moi—I don't recall seeing Finnegan, my family's name, on any publicly traded stocks, or published in *Forbes*, or published *ever*, for that matter. Okay, maybe in a scholarly quarterly journal or something, but certainly not in the glossy party pictures of *Vogue* or *Town & Country*, where I regularly spied my classmates' moms in their couture designer duds.

Luckily, I don't really have to deal with all the over-the-top craziness of my own Sweet Sixteen. See, when I talk about these parties, I'm not talking about pizza and Pepsi at the local bowling alley. I mean black tie. I mean hotel ballrooms and flowers and lighting schemes and bands; events that cost more than a down payment for a small house in Ronkonkoma. But because my parents are NYU professors and barely have enough dough to have a Chuck E. Cheese fete, freaking about having the best bash isn't even an option. Don't get me wrong; it's not like I'm on welfare or anything, but my parents can't even pay twenty grand a year for tuition at Tate on their teacher's salaries, so they obviously are not going to cough up half a mill on a rager that lasts a few hours. And although I admit that sometimes I like to imagine what sort of multimillion-dollar soiree I would host if I had the chance, honestly, seeing how everyone was wigging over hatching their gilded plans made it a little easier to be poor.

So this autumn, when we all returned to school, I was prepared to ignore all the party-planning brouhaha and just dive into my textbooks and chalk up some A's so I had a decent chance of a scholarship to an Ivy. The morning crunch of girls packed our class lounge, snapping cell phones shut, hanging up Gucci overcoats, and unpacking their Prada book bags into their closets. I said hi and greeted some of my classmates, asking breezily about their summers and hearing their litany of whirlwind adventures and world travel—one skied in the Alps, one attended summer classes at Le Rosée in Switzerland, one worked with "youths" in inner-city Chicago by day (then checked in to sleep at the Drake Hotel by night), and one hot-air ballooned through Scandinavia. Me, I worked at a camp in Maine teaching sewing in the crafts department and had fun but was psyched to come home and see my friends. Most of all, my best friend, Whitney.

Whitney Blake is pretty much perfect. But not annoyingly perfect, just effortlessly flawless. Buttery blond and blue-eyed with Waspy facial architecture that Michelangelo would have used as a blueprint for his next statue, she was christened in Baby Dior, summered in Southampton, and sampled her first potato galette with caviar at age seven. I know, it sounds nuts, but it's all she's ever known, and she's actually really down to earth. Otherwise, I wouldn't be friends with her. We bonded from day one when she complimented my French braid in second grade, and since I am an only child and she has an older brother she never sees, we became almost like sisters. She never made a big deal about my non-glam background; in fact, she loves my fam—and the fact that my house is normal, happy, and chill. If her parents are jet set, mine are sofa set: mellow, book reading, and always relaxed. Whitney and I just get each other the way old friends do; we complete each other's thoughts and sentences; it's like we have a code.

We do have our differences; I can get stressed out (schoolwork, parents, life) and she's usually very calm and confident.

That's because when you've pretty much been the queen bee for as long as anyone can remember, no one tries to dethrone you. The whole Sweet Sixteen thing? Not a thorn in Whit's side—she and everyone else knew her January party would blow everyone else's out of the Evian. She's not cocky about it; she just knows. Like with guys. They *woooor*ship her. I mean, putty in her manicured hands. They circle around her like sharks on the prowl for her size-four chum.

Whit and I see each other every day and talk every night. Still, we always come to school and gather with our posse (our two other best friends, Kaitlin and Ava) to catch up on any other gossip that has gone down in the hours since we last convened. So today, after staking out our tenth-grade quarters and locating our new digs, Whit and I rendezvoused at ten of eight in the lounge.

"He called me last night."

I turned around from my closet at Whitney's elated morning report and got an excited jolt as if it were a hot guy calling *me*. I mean, I've had minor hookups and stuff, but with my un-Barbie looks (brown hair, brown eyes, kinda pale, and, oh yeah, small boobs) I am hardly schoolboy drool material. But I do love hearing Whit's romantic stories. We always get psyched for each other about everything—guys, grades (guys for her, grades for me, alas, study-dork that I am), and we always mutually support. I'd been waiting to hear if she aced her latest game of flirt-o-rama. He had called.

"He is so effing *hot*, Laura! I mean, like, *en fuego*. He's thinking of becoming a male model. He's been approached by, like, Abercrombie's scouts."

After a summer of beachside clambakes, tennis lessons, and heavy petting with the Greystone Country Club lifeguard, Whit was on a high. But before she could launch into full recap, Kaitlin approached with Ava and they kissed each of us on both cheeks, the usual Euro-style greeting all the girls at Tate gave one another in the mornings.

"Hey, girleens," said Ava, running off. "I've gotta bolt and go get a new chick downstairs to tour her around. See you later." Ava was the girl who was extracurricularing herself into college. She was a tour guide, worked in the admissions office, was on student council, had a column called "Cappuccinos and Conversation" in the *Tate Gazette*, and had just become secretary of the French Club (she was partial to Louis Vuitton). With her giant apple-green eyes and her chic little Frédéric Fekkai–snipped bob, she was the epitome of a Tate student, which is probably why she was on the cover of the Tate bulletin every quarter.

"So, what's this I overheard about your beach boy becoming a male model?" Kaitlin asked, rolling her eyes.

"What's wrong with that?" asked Whitney. "I mean, helloo! He's stunning."

"Whatever." Kaitlin shrugged, flipped her strawberry blond hair, and walked off to plop her Chanel quilted tote and cashmere sweater-coat in her closet. Whitney looked at me with a perfectly plucked raised brow.

"Laura, what do you think? You always tell me the truth." Whitney leaned in closer. "I mean, I love Kaitlin, but she always says these little barbed things and then walks off and won't tell me what she's really thinking."

"Whit, you are smart," I started. "And I tend to think of male models as vapid himbo types who are really vain. I know he's older and ripped and stuff, but come on, do you really want a guy who counts calories more than you? Lame-*issimo*."

"Oh my God, you are so right," she said, fidgeting with her signet ring. "That would fully freak me out." She twisted a lock of her hair. "Plus I still love our gang of guys at Bradley. Jake Watkins totally has a thing for me, I can sense it. Maybe I should go for him this year," she said, pondering.

"Jake Watkins?" I asked, surprised. I didn't know Whitney was into Jake. I didn't know she had really even noticed him. I mean, he was the hottest of the Bradley gang, but last year we had been hanging more with the St. Peter's guys and had only recently decided to clean house and bring the Bradley boys into the forefront of our lives. I had known Jake from ballroom dancing school and always casually chatted with him at Youth Against Cancer dances. Although I knew he went to Southampton during the summer, I had no idea that he was on Whitney's radar. "I just . . . I didn't know you liked him."

"Oh yeah, we hung out in Southampton. He's had a total growth spurt over the summer, and he literally makes Orlando Bloom look like a barfburger. I am totally going to lock him in this year. I mean, right? Don't you think he's better than the male model?" she asked, looking at me earnestly.

"Totally. Smart is better. You have to remember," I instructed, "male models are like Cadbury Cream Eggs: The outside shell is really sweet, but inside there's nothing but goo." Ah well. Another hottie had been claimed by Whit. Usually I didn't even know the guys Whit liked, but Jake . . .

Whitney burst out laughing. "I missed your special Laura lingo this summer," she said, putting her arm around me. There is no one like you, suga."

That was true, at least in Whitney's life. I think what bonded us together so well was that I am very matter-of-fact; I tell it like it is, no bull malarkey. And although Whitney did love the sycophants who were all too happy to kiss her Prada butt, I think she realized that she needed me, the one person who knew her inside and out and wouldn't let her get away with anything. We made a good team. And now I guess she and Jake would make a good team also.

Whitney looked around confidently and did a signature Whit Blake hair flip. "I feel it in my bones," she said, beaming as she visually drank in her domain. "This year is gonna rock."

Suddenly, from the threshold of the lounge door came a very loud burst of unfamiliar laughter. It wasn't accidental, spontaneous laughter but attention-getting laughter. Every perfectly groomed head in the room whipped around.

"You're so funny, Ava!" the offender boomed before realizing the lounge was pin-drop silent and her voice sounded like someone had put a microphone implant in her throat. She turned to Ava, stage-whispering audibly, "Geez, it's like a mortuary in here. Doesn't anyone talk?"

Ava laughed. "It's still early, sweetie. We haven't had our lattes yet."

"Well, I hope that's all it is, because this place is seeming pretty deadsville," she sniffed.

"Come on, let me show you your closet," said Ava, leading the girl to the corner.

I turned to Whitney and noticed her eyes digesting every detail about this girl with utter contempt. I looked back and a little five-alarm fire bell went off in my head: We were going to have a problem. She was the antithesis of Whitney. Her hair, although blond, was kind of messy and more of a brassy color, with exposed roots that seemed contrived rather than careless. She had very white teeth and very plump lips and flashed a million-dollar smile when she laughed—which was every five seconds. Although clad in the requisite Tate uniform, she had already boldly made it her own, tailoring her skirt way above the knees, pulling her white oxford ever so tight around her suspiciously ample boobs, and draping tons of Lance Armstrong cancer bracelets on her wrist. (Hey! Make a fashion statement *and* fight cancer!) Her shoes were the latest Louis Vuittons that had been photographed everywhere, and she wore giant diamond-and-gold studs that looked suspiciously like the ones J. Lo had worn to the Golden Globes. It was funny, because even though her eyes were slightly small for her face, and she wasn't the thinnest person I had ever seen, she had something else: She was sexy. Yes, she definitely had that dirty-girl thing going for her, which guys were going to lap up with a spoon. And you could tell in one swoop by the way she made her audacious entrance into our school that she was someone who loved to be the center of attention. Bring on the red flags right now.

"Who the hell is *that*?" Whitney sneered, her voice oozing with disgust.

"You haven't met the new girl yet?" asked Kaitlin, hastily making her way over from her closet. She always liked to be in on everything. "I rode up with her in the 'vator. Cute, right?"

"I haven't met her," said Whitney.

"Me neither," I muttered.

"Oh my God, she's, like, *really* cool. She's from L.A. It's so awesome, because we haven't had a cool new girl in *years*," said Kaitlin, smiling appraisingly in the girl's direction.

"What's her name?" I asked.

"Sophie Mitchum. Her dad is Marty Mitchum," said Kaitlin knowingly.

"Who the eff is that?" asked Whitney.

"Duh!" said Kaitlin, exasperated. "He produced, like, every major movie you've seen for the past ten years. And Sophie knows soooo many celebs." Kaitlin leaned in conspiratorially, her gold Elsa Peretti heart necklace dangling like a pendulum in my face. "She literally has Kirsten Dunst's cell number and Chad Michael Murray's pager."

Whitney rolled her eyes. "She already told you that? Talk about trying too hard."

"Oh, Whit! Be nice. I mean, if I get to meet Chad it will be *beyond.* Anyhoo, I promised her I'd show her where the science lab is, so later."

Kaitlin rushed over to Sophie, who already had a small gaggle of potential friends surrounding her. She had whipped a Gucci picture holder out of her Hogan bag and was showing aerial photos of her manse in Beverly Hills. Tack.

"God, I forgot how juvenile everyone is here," sighed Whitney. "I mean, I was hanging out with an older crowd this summer, and I'm sooo not used to this."

"Sorry, Miss Belle-of-the-Senior-Citizen-Ball," I teased, calling Whitney out on her attitude. "We're too fetal for you."

Whitney smiled at me. "Shut up. You know I'm not talking about you. You're the only one I can deal with here."

"Come on, let's go learn about rolling heads in France," I said, taking her arm and leading her to history class.

Throughout the morning, Whitney and Sophie were like two dogs, sniffing each other out, watching every move—the two most gorgeous girls each trying to see where the social chips would fall. I think it was what people refer to as a Mexican standoff. Whitney's pretty territorial and doesn't take well to potential rivals. And as the day trickled on, I could tell that Sophie was the same way. Here we had a classic evolution problem: two queen bees, one hive. But in our class of only forty-one girls, it was inevitable that at some point the titans had to clash.

It didn't take long for Sophie to figure out that Whitney held the throne of the social court. During badminton, Whitney was telling Ava about her lifeguard while Sophie watched, curious. I saw her scope Whit's Cartier tank watch and Tiffany studs, and it was clear she knew this gal was a fashion leader of the pack.

Then, in the science lab, Whit's eyebrow arched ever so slightly as Sophie giggled flirtatiously with Mr. Everwood, the hottie teacher (who, rumor had it, had banged a senior the year before). *Sophie = cute but semi-cheese, non?* said the note that Whitney scribbled and slid across to me in English class. I tried to read it discreetly and nod sympathetically while keeping my head erect and my eyes focused on Mr. Houser, who was droning on and on about the brilliance of nineteenth-century Russian authors.

I could see, out of the corner of my eye, Whitney glaring at Sophie, who was taking copious notes in her monogrammed leather-bound notebook. That morning I had observed in classes that I shared with Sophie that she had plastered snapshots of herself with various celebrities on the inside flaps of her textbooks and folders and would glide her finger along the photos every so often, causing every eye in the class to follow her nails running up and down Brad Pitt or Jessica Simpson's beaming face. It was a surefire way to get noticed, as well as to annoy the hell out of Whit. Every time she did it, Whit would thrust another note on my lap (*Could she be more of a star worshiper?* Gag), and I would cringe in fear of getting busted by the teacher. They were pretty strict about that stuff at Tate.

Just as Mr. Houser took a pause from his introductory rant on Dostoyevsky, Sophie's hand shot up.

"Yes, Miss Mitchum?" asked Mr. Houser, who, with his sad brown suit and mustard-colored mustache, always looked beaten down and surprised when anyone paid attention to him.

"Hi. Since I'm new, I'm not sure how it all goes down here, but my father, Marty Mitchum, is like dear, *dear* friends with Julie Christie, and she was in *Doctor Zhivago*, so if you, like, want her to come in to class to discuss that book, 'cause I know it was written by Dostoyevsky, I can totally arrange it."

Mr. Houser looked surprised. "That's very generous, Sophie. Actually *Doctor Zhivago* is by Boris Pasternak and is twentieth-century Russian literature, which we will be studying next year."

Now, *I* would have been totally mortified, but not Sophie.

"Oh, well then, let's plan for next year. Maybe we can all go to Russian Samovar for lunch with her—Baryshnikov owns it and he's, like, another great friend of my dad's."

I couldn't resist turning to look at Whitney, whose eyes widened in shock.

On our way to lunch, Whitney let loose. "Three words: tacky, tacky, *tacky*!"

"Shh . . . she'll totally hear you."

"I don't care. She is yucksville. Could she name-drop any more? I mean, I've never even talked to her personally and I know that Mr. Chow is 'like her kitchen,' that they moved here because her dad was making a trilogy with 'Marty'—not even Martin, but

Marty—Scorsese, and that the guy who played the dad on *7th Heaven* is her godfather. Barf."

"Yeah, she's really something." I wasn't sure what to make of Sophie, actually. She both repelled and compelled me. On the one hand she was a brazen name-dropper, but on the other she seemed unabashed about it, and that was kind of refreshing. It could get irritating when someone at Tate tried to brag in subtle whispers that they had dined with Henry Kissinger the night before, but then had to give all these disclaimers like they don't care about famous people, blah, blah, blah. *Yeah, right.*

The jury was still out on Miss Mitchum. Lunch seemed like a good opportunity for further deliberation.

Chapter Three

Our dining room is not your average scene with a lunch lady in a hairnet glopping spoonfuls of tragic meats and powdered potatoes on trays. I'm talking Dutch still-life-worthy cornucopias of gourmet Dean & Deluca–catered smorgasbords. I'm talking Italian soda fountains, towers of fresh bagels, a freshly squeezed juice bar, and a thirty-foot salad bar with over sixty ingredients and two Malaysian choppers who slice 'n' dice out designer lunches in large bowls and toss them with mini–sterling ladles of fat-free dressing. The wallpaper is the same as in the dining room in Buckingham Palace, a floral chinoiserie with some birds on it, handmade, like, a hundred years ago.

We sat down with our china plates at our usual white tablecloth-covered haunt, in the back left corner, as far away from the faculty table as humanly possible. We had started eating when, suddenly, Whitney looked up and stared across the dining room. Uh-oh: *Jaws* music should have been playing in the background as our soundtrack. Sophie had walked out with a plate of . . . grapes. Just grapes. And she was scanning the tables to see where to plop her Pilates'd bum. Just then, Ava waved.

"Stop it, Ava!" Whitney chided her in a harsh whisper. "Don't have her come here. *Quelle idiote!*"

"Whit, she's cool, I swear," she replied, smiling up at Sophie, who was already halfway across the room, approaching at mach-ten speed.

"Great," Whit said, shooting me a look.

Sophie came up to us with a huge smile. It was hard to dislike someone who was so friendly.

"Hi! I haven't met some of you guys yet. I'm Sophie Mitchum."

"Hi, I'm Laura Finnegan," I answered. "Nice to meet you."

There was a small pause. I continued. "And this is Whitney Blake."

"Hi," Whit said, semi-coldly. Brrr! But Sophie took it in stride.

"It's so nice to meet you! Can I sit with you?"

Ava, Kaitlin, and I all erupted in "absolutely"s and "sure, sure, sure!"s while Whit just ate her balsamic-splattered frisée.

"I looove that Tiffany bean necklace," Sophie said, looking at Whitney.

"Oh, thanks."

Whitney kicked me under the table. It was our secret mode o' communication. Sometimes I swear my shin is black and blue thanks to all the nudges from her pointed toes.

"Actually," Sophie continued, beaming at Whitney, "I saw Lindsay Lohan in the dressing room at Fred Segal, and she had the same one, so chic. God, I miss Fred Segal! You guys'll have to show me the cool shopping here. I have zero winter clothing! Except for, like, the ski outfits I wear in Aspen."

"Well, Whitney knows all the great stores," I said, trying to bring my arctic best friend into the conversational fold. It was so lame when she was rude for no reason, which tended to happen from time to time when Whit felt threatened. I mean, hey, Sophie was trying; give her a break. "She could replace Robert Verdi on the Style Network's *Fashion Police.*"

"Ew," said Whitney, hitting my arm teasingly. "Verdi is so cheese. Hello, Gouda! He'd win the gold medal in the tacky Olympics. And besides," she said, looking Sophie in the eye for the first time, "Laura is so our style setter."

"Totally," agreed Kaitlin. "She can in one nano make a lameoid outfit look trendy and hip."

"You guys!" I said, embarrassed but flattered.

Sophie looked at me and nodded. "I can totally tell you are emitting a killer style vibe." Then she turned to Whitney, knowing by now she was the tougher nut to crack. "And you—you are totally channeling Mischa Barton. You guys are, like, twins separated at birth!"

Ladies and gentlemen, Point One for Miss Mitchum. This clearly registered well with Whit because I happen to know she thinks Mischa is überchic and one of the only young stars that passes red carpet muster with us (no tacky cleavage, no whorefest getups). I could see Whitney brighten. But the thaw would not come that easily. See, Whitney is pretty black and white about everything. She loves you or hates you. Something's either "totally in" or "soooo out." Whitney would keep playing hard to get until she could pass a positive verdict on Sophie.

"Well, I'm not sure about that," said Whit, still not completely ready to concede. "Mischa is pretty chic, but unfortch still has a little bit of that California thing going on. No offense." She smiled enigmatically at Sophie. I could see Sophie still had some work to do. Whitney wanted to make absolutely sure that she knew who was the ruler of our little fiefdom. (I had always considered myself consigliere, which was fine by me.)

"None taken. All of us from the coast have our own style, which is often misunderstood by the rest of the world. Except for Donatella Versace. She says she gets all her inspiration from Angelinos," said Sophie, who didn't seem to bristle at all from Whitney's semijab.

"Well, Donatella is not exactly what I would call *chic*," began Whitney.

"You're right, Sophie," I said, trying to avoid a style debate. "Los Angeles style may as well be martian style for us stiffs in the Big Apple. We're pretty reserved."

"I can tell. The headmistress gave me daggers when she saw how tight my shirt was. Do they, like, want us to forget that we have boobs? Why don't they just suit us up in nuns' outfits and strap them down?" said Sophie.

"That's for the convent girls across the street," said Ava, laughing.

"Well, a sinner like me will never be able to darken the doors of a convent," giggled Sophie.

Sophie seemed to have passed muster with Whit, at least for now. By the end of lunch, even Whitney was cracking a smile at some of Sophie's jokes.

I stayed late after school to meet with our Russian teacher, Mrs. Federov, to talk about organizing a Russian club. As I was packing my gigantic book bag in the lounge, Sophie came out of Madame Hurley's office, looking a little flustered. Uh-oh. Madame Hurley was the head of Upper School and known to be kind of intimidating. Sophie smiled when she saw me.

"Hey," she said, trying to put on a chipper voice. I could tell that this was not the cheerful and confident Sophie that I had seen a few hours before.

"Hey, Sophie. How's it going?" I asked.

"Oh, just amazing, thanks," she said, burying her head in her cabinet so that I wouldn't notice the tearstains on her cheeks.

I walked over to her. I felt totally bad, remembering the first time I went to camp and felt like a total outsider. It was a bummer to be the new kid on the block, that's for sure. "It must be really sucky starting a new school and everything."

She turned and looked at me and smiled with total sincerity. "It is . . . it's just, soooo different from my school in L.A. I mean, in L.A. we could call the teachers by their first names and we had boys!!! It was really more like a giant premiere. But here . . ."

"I know, it's hardly a festive atmosphere," I said, smiling. "But don't worry, Sophie. You'll do fine once you get the hang of it."

She took a deep breath. "I guess . . ."

"You will," I said, suddenly giving her a reassuring hug.

"Thanks, Laura."

We walked out of the building together and I filled her in on all the teachers, who to avoid, who to get as an advisor, and the whole scandal with the previous piano teacher. I could tell she cheered up a little as we walked, and we hugged again before we set off on our separate ways.

"One more thing," she said before we departed. "How do I get through to the queen bee?"

"Whitney?" I asked, surprised.

"Yeah. I can tell that it's her fiefdom and I totally appreciate that. I was like that at my old school. But I think we could all be friends. I just don't want her to feel threatened, because I won't step on her toes."

I smiled. Sophie was smart—she had totally nailed Whitney in one day. "Um, maybe come bearing gifts?" I suggested.

"Done," said Sophie, smiling.

I liked Sophie. She was flashy and brassy, but there was a chewy center to her. I hoped we could be friends.

On the phone that night, Whitney and I recapped the day.

"So what are we thinking about L.A. chick?" Whit asked. I could practically hear her twirling her hair through the phone, her trademark *I'm thinking long and hard* gesture.

I decided not to tell her about Sophie's confession and display of vulnerability. I don't know, I just felt like it was a private moment that Whitney didn't need to dissect.

"You know what?" I said. "I really like her. At first the jury was out, and I thought maybe she was a little vacuous, but I don't think so now. She's cool."

"I hear that," Whitney said, considering this. "But I'm still not sure. She could be our next best friend or the suckiest bi-atch ever. I haven't decided yet." Like I said, extremes.

The next day, I knew by first period that Sophie was going to power through Whit's black-and-white spectrum to gleaming white when she entered the lounge with four tiny shopping bags with little striped ribbons.

"Hi, gals," she said as we were unpacking our book bags into our closets. "Prezzies for my nuevo pals!" She gave us each a little Olive and Bette's tissue-stuffed bag, in which we found small chocolate-brown leather pouches with our initials in pink. Pretty cute. I looked up at her and she winked at me. "I saw these and just couldn't resist."

"Oh! I worship this!" squealed Ava, hugging Sophie. "Thanks, love!"

Kaitlin and I thanked her, too, as our eyes turned to Whitney to gauge her reaction.

She looked at the cute lowercase *w* and then up at a beaming Sophie. "I almost bought this at Olive and Bette's, but they were totally sold out. They're so hard to find," she said, looking at Sophie gratefully. "J'adore."

The 'bergs of Whit's cold front melted away as we all admired our matching new accessories. I could tell our posse had a new member.

"I'd love to go do Madison after badminton. We can find you a cute shearling at Searle, Sophie," said Whitney.

"I'd love that!" beamed Sophie.

"Hid," sighed Whitney when Sophie popped out of the dressing room to model a dark brown coat. "What do you think, Laura?"

Sophie twirled around. I walked over and tied the belt. "Well, I think it's just too boxy, not well made. It makes you look a little stocky, which is obviously *insane* because you are like Lindsay Lohan, so I think you should try on the other one."

"Why can't I just get a little mink coat?" asked Sophie. "That's what I had for Aspen. I mean, I've outgrown it now, but I could get the next size—"

"No, no, no," Whitney and I said in unison. "Teenagers can't do the fur thing," Whitney said solemnly.

"But isn't shearling fur?" asked Sophie.

"Yes and no," I said.

"Mink's too gauche," said Whitney. "Flashy."

"Okay, I trust you guys," said Sophie, retreating to the three-way mirror across the room. "But all these rules seem so bizarre! I mean, the point is to stay warm and look fabulous, isn't it?"

As she disappeared to try on the next possibility, Whitney and I exchanged smiles. Our new friend needed a lot of help, and that was good news for Whitney. I think she sensed Sophie was hardly a wall-flower in her old school but that she'd need assistance acclimating to her new world. Our world, where Whitney was in charge.

"Ta-da!" said Sophie, jumping out of the dressing room in a camel-colored coat.

"Perfection," pronounced Whitney.

I went over and pulled down the sleeves a little and knotted the belt. "Yes, this one's good," I said, nodding.

"Finally!" said Sophie, excited. "Now, how many should I get? Three? How about the black and the chocolate and the cream, too?"

"Whoa." Whitney's eyes nearly popped out of her head. "You only need one."

"One? I'm supposed to wear the same coat every day?" asked Sophie, shocked.

"If it does the job," I said.

"That seems so weird. People *do* that?" asked Sophie, still perplexed.

"You're only wearing it from the door of your house to the front door of your car, and then from the car to the school. Who's going to notice?" I said.

"Everybody only has one," Whitney said with assurance.

Sophie was still skeptical. "Okay, I'll just get one for now, but maybe next week we'll regroup and go on the hunt for another. It seems weird, one coat! My parents will literally have coronaries when they see how restrained I was. But I trust you—you guys are so chic. Laura, where did you get that rad outfit you're wearing?"

"Actually, I made it," I said with a mixture of embarrassment and pride.

"Get out!" boomed Sophie so loudly that two salesgirls in the front frowned at us.

My ultimate passion was clothing design. In my dreams I would fully head toward a career as the next Karl Lagerfeld. And I had become more than handy with a needle, if I do say so myself. It wasn't just a financial thing, although it did help to make your own duds when you can't slam down the plastique like Whit and Sophie. But more important, it was my "artistic outlet," as Whitney described it. And she was right. I was way into it. I wish I had the focus or the time or the guts to actually design a line for people other than myself, but I was too scared to try it. For now it was just couture for one.

"Laura makes all of her clothes," said Whitney, beaming. "She's the *most* amazing designer. Like if you see something in a magazine, she can totally reproduce it and tailor anything you need. Oscar de la Renta comes to our annual Christmas party and I'm going to bombard him with Laura's sketchbook. He'll *freak*."

"That's so wicked. You are a total Stella McCartney. How did you learn to do that?"

"I've been sewing since I was five. At first I thought it was totally D.A., but now I've gotten really into it."

"D.A.? District Attorney?" asked Sophie, confused.

"No, Dorks Anonymous," I said. Whitney and I had created our own little lingo.

"That's such a cool phrase. I totally have to use that the next time I see my pals from the coast; they'll get a real laugh out of it," said Sophie. "But wow, I am way impressed with your look. I mean, how chic is Laura? Total inner style."

"Her stuff is way better than everything at Scoop or Incubator," said Whitney. I swear, I should put Whitney on the payroll for her praise. She was totally supportive, almost like a stage mother.

"Are those stores?" asked Sophie.

"The hippest in New York," said Whitney.

"You'll have to take me there for sure," said Sophie, heading to the cash register with her new purchase.

"Obvy," said Whitney.

"You guys are so great," said Sophie, slapping down an American Express black card on the counter. "I'm in a really good space here. I was so nauseous about being the loser new girl slash foreign exchange student, so I'm way glad I found my power clique!"

"She's just fun to have around. Granted, she is a little name-droppy, but hey, at least she's generous with her celeb gossip." I was sitting at my kitchen table eating dinner with my parents and telling them all about Sophie. "She and Whit also have fully bonded. I swear, their salesgirl today was on cloud nine because their credit cards had quite a workout." I paused, knowing my parents hated talk of material things. It was so not our fam. "But I really like Sophie; I'm psyched to have a new pal in our gang."

"That's wonderful, darling," said my mom, reaching over to the refrigerator to grab more milk. Our little yellow kitchen was tiny ("charming," my mother called it), so our dinners were pretty informal. Cartons on the table, our seventeen-year-old cat Buster on my father's lap, and the *New York Times* Sunday crossword under my mother's plate were not uncommon. Whitney's parents, the incredibly formal Mr. and Mrs. Peyton Rockingham Blake III, who could slash their wrists and have blue blood seep out and ruin their Oriental carpet, would have been *horrified* at our fourth-floor walk-up digs. We had piles upon piles of books—not just on the countless shelves lining the walls but on every imaginable surface. My mom's math corkboard was covered in proofs for her lecture the next day, and the giant manila envelope of clippings my dad had saved for me to read leaned against the couch (he was always saving editorials he thought would interest me), along with his basket of *New Republic* back issues. It was haphazard but pure Finnegan.

"Sophie's family is in the film business? How fascinating," said my father.

"Yeah, she knows everyone. She's literally having dinner tonight with the Olsen twins."

"Are they a rock and roll band?" asked my mother.

"No." I sighed. "They're . . . never mind."

My parents live in their own solar system and have no idea what goes on in the pages of *Us Weekly.* They were both in their early forties when they had me, so they are already gray-haired intellectuals, so to speak (my dad still has a huge head of thick, dark hair), close to senior citizenship at this stage of their life. Both are in surprisingly good shape, though, probably because they have to haul arse up all those floors every day to our walk-up. Our little triumvirate has always been a team, and they've always treated me as an adult (read: no curfew, which makes my classmates beyond jealous). Both of them are professors at New York University—my mother is in the math department and my father teaches philosophy (an extremely useful subject. Not!). They're basically aging hippie brainiac types who have lived in the same two-bedroom bursting-at-the-seams-with-towers-upon-towers-of-books rent-stabilized apartment in the West Village for twenty years.

"Sophie already promised she'd have her dad name characters after us in his next movie. How cool is that?"

"Are they some sort of athletic team?" asked my mother.

"Who?"

"The Olsen twins?" she said, pulling at her beaded necklace.

"No, Mom, and we've moved beyond that conversation already. Anyway, the awesome thing is that Sophie just clicked with Whit, Kaitlin, Ava, and me," I said, getting up to clear my plate. I dumped the remnants of my broccoli, corn, and meat loaf (barf!) into the garbage.

"That's wonderful, dear," said my father, wiping gravy off his tweed jacket. He always somehow manages to spill something or other all over himself when he eats. Usually it was because he was so distracted. Definitely the "absentminded professor."

"Oh my gosh!" I said, slapping myself on the head. "I can't believe I didn't think of this sooner! This means I'll have one more *major* Sweet Sixteen party to go to!"

Both of my parents looked at me quizzically. "Is that good or bad?" my father said, cocking his head.

"It's both. I mean, it's awesome, but that means I need to make one more dress for myself. Between all these parties, plus the Gold and Silver Ball in December, I am going to be in sewing overdrive."

There was no doubt that Sophie would have a major blowout. In fact, I bet her party might even rival Whitney's, with all her Hollywood connections.

Chapter Five

That Saturday, after I finished jamming on all my homework, I went to meet up with Whit and Sophie. I know, I know, I am such a big fat loser to study on Saturdays, but Sundays make me want to hurl when I wake up and eat brunch and have piles o' slaveitude, so I'd rather get it over with.

While teasing me mercilessly for my dorkissima ways, we hit the downtown shopping scene, i.e., my turf. See, most girls at Tate break into hives when they have to leave their glam 10021 zip code; many people, despite the fact that they live in such a colorful and amazing city as the Big Apple, never leave their Bentley-lined 'hood. Around seventh grade it became cooler to explore downtown, but sometimes I still bristle at the invisible stigma that I'm some Oliver Twist urchin living in gritty Bohemia. In fifth grade my mom planned a party for me at our apartment, and not one, not two, but *five* moms called to ask for driving directions. I mean, hellllooo? New York is a grid, people! This one mom asked, "Where is West Ninth Street?" and my mom said, "Between Eighth and Tenth Streets."

Anyway, the cool thing about Whitney versus many of the Dolce-clad drones in my class is that she had always been game to explore, and ever since I introduced Whit to my all-time fave boutique, Incubator, she's been obsessed. It's basically the coolest store in the city—all young, hip designers, fresh out of Parsons or FIT, and if you buy something there, you won't see everyone wearing it. Tons of the designers now lining the racks of Barney's all started there, and the owner, Jade, is my idol.

"She's gorgeous," Sophie whispered as she stared at Jade.

"Oh, drop dead," replied Whitney as we watched Jade chat on the phone, running a hand through her jet black glossy straight hair. "She used to be a model, and then she quit to be with this rocker guy in Williamsburg; so hot."

"We've totally shrined her," I added. "There was an article on her in *Vogue*, and she styles all these music videos now."

"Wow," said Sophie, wide-eyed. "She's so edgy and chic; love her!"

Jade waved and gestured she'd just be another minute on the phone.

"What time does the band come on?" Jade said, jotting on a notepad. "Killer."

She hung up and sighed, turning to us. "Hey, girlies." She came out from behind the counter and kissed Whitney and me.

"Jade, this is our friend Sophie," I said.

"Hey," said Jade, shaking her hand.

"This is *such* a fab place!" gushed Sophie. "It's so cool and modern, but there's this, like, vintage-y vibe!"

"You know my chocolate brown velvet jacket I was wearing the other day?" Whitney asked Sophie. "That was from here."

"Your clothes are all to keel over and die for," said Sophie. "I am sooo about to do some serious damage!"

The phone rang and Jade turned to grab it. "We have other sizes in the back, too, so let me know if you need anything."

"I sooo love her aura!" said Sophie.

"I know, she rules, right?" said Whitney.

"Okay: now, Laura," Sophie said, looking at me very seriously. "Since this is your find, what pieces do you recommend for my spree?"

"Everything here is pretty much spot-on in terms of major originality," I said, drinking in the amazing racks of clothes I sadly could never buy. "Jade was the first to really embrace the whole Japanese scene. You can't find this level of cut, tailoring, and detail in many places."

Sophie was in drool mode, a fit of orgasmic shopper's delight. "Oh my God, Mission Control to planet Amex! We need you!" Sophie said as she loaded her thin arms with piles of clothes. "I have that wave where I just know I'm about to drop megabucks."

"Well, you're in the best place." I smiled.

"Now listen, you guys, we have to fully stock up on red-carpet-worthy loot! Get out your BlackBerries," Sophie said, looking at us with a raised brow. "Friday you have to come with me to my dad's friend Quentin's movie premiere at the Ziegfeld!"

"No way," I said, floored. Whoa. Would my life really be that *Entertainment Tonight*?

"Way," answered Sophie. "I just asked Daddy this morning if I could bring you guys and he said yes! We're getting a limo and everything!"

"Awesome!" squealed Whitney. "I am so trying on this cutie frock," she said, marching into the dressing room.

"Laura," said Sophie, turning my way before hitting the dressing room herself. "Aren't you gonna try anything on? I'm feeling those lacey chemises are so you!"

"Oh, no, I'm all set," I said, somewhat self-consciously, as my two pals tore off their outfits behind the deep-purple curtains.

Ninety minutes and God knows how much dough later, we were out on Avenue A and I was helping Whitney and Sophie find a cab to share uptown; we were all sleeping over at Whitney's house that night, and I had to stop home to pack my bag.

"Thanks, sweets!" gushed Sophie, putting her arm around

me. "That was such a blast. We are totally ready for our close-up!"

A cab pulled up and they loaded in with their garment bags galore.

"Okay, Lo-lo," Whitney said, giving me a hug. "Soph and I will see you at my place in a couple hours—"

The cab drove off, and through the window I saw them laughing. I couldn't help but feel the tiniest sting of, well, this is majorly embarrassing slash insecure but . . . weirdo jealousy? I mean, normally Whitney would come over with me and wait while I packed and then we'd ride up together. But today she had Sophie to share a cab with and was suddenly splitsville. And not only that, Sophie had totally stepped in as her buying buddy because she could match her credit limit. Was I being replaced? No, no, no, I was being silly. How could I ever feel excluded because of a dumb shopping spree and the fact that they both lived uptown? Whitney and I were best friends. And Sophie was really fun. Three isn't a crowd—that was just bull, and I got annoyed at myself for even having such a random, immature thought. I tried to banish it from my head immediately. *Three is not a crowd! Three is not a crowd!* Right?

Chapter Six

Unlike my house, where you just have to call up—and because our intercom doesn't work we buzz anyone in (probably knife-wielding serial killers)—getting into Whitney's Park Avenue pad was like trying to penetrate the Pentagon. I had to give my name to the first doorman, pass inspection from the second doorman, cruise up to the fifteenth floor with the ancient elevator man (I mean, I think I could handle pressing a button), and then go through a series of maids and butlers that opened various doors until I finally found my friend.

Adela, the Blakes' uniformed El Salvadorian maid, opened the grand mahogany front door to let me into the apartment.

"Hi, Adela," I said.

"Hi, Miss Laura," she said, taking my coat. I had always felt a little weird about letting Whitney's "help," as she called them, defrock me. What am I, paralyzed? But when I saw that my resistance only got the staff in trouble and accused of laziness, I had decided to relent.

I walked across the black-and-white marbled floor and veered left down a long taupe-colored hallway lined with Matisse collages. The Blakes had the most fantastic art collection, so awesome that we even went to their house on class trips to study the Dutch masters. It sure beat the posters of famous philosophers and family snapshots in simple black frames that my parents had slapped on our walls. In fact, the Blakes' apartment was the exact opposite of mine: Instead of squeaky wooden floorboards they had thick, plush wall-to-wall carpeting in earth tones that muted out any noises (the whole family would rather be neither seen nor heard). Our walls are painted bright colors and could probably use a paint job (chips were cropping up everywhere), and their walls had expensive wallpaper—some toile, some floral, some with weird bird scenes, and even some with cashmere! All of their furniture was antique—it's like all the hard work that Louis XIV's and Louis XV's carpenters did in France a century or two ago ended up on Seventy-first and Park, right in Whit's house. What we considered antique in our house was my father's desk, which he bought in 1974, and which had a scratch in it that made it look older. We really couldn't be more opposite.

"Hey, Whit," I said, turning into Whitney's gi-normous bedroom. I don't envy anything Whit has, but I have to admit I could totally deal with her room. It's all decorated in a subtle sage green $300-a-yard chintz—everything from the window seat and the thick drapes to the bench at the foot of her canopy bed. She has an overstuffed sofa and armchair at the other end of her room in a soft printed white-on-white fabric, with cashmere ivory Ralph Lauren throws to curl up in while watching TV. The whole room is compartmentalized in the most amazing way: One nook is for TV viewing. Another nook, her magazine collection—arranged by theme (*Cosmo Girl!*, *Teen Vogue!*)—is as organized as a *Hold Everything* catalog. In another nook is her "workstation," which holds her Chippendale desk, her brand-new iMac computer, and my favorite of all: her stationery collection. I am such a sucker for nice papers. Whenever I pass a stationery store, I just have to do a drive-by. And Whit has all of her hand-engraved letterhead, envelopes, business cards (Who needs those at age fifteen? Not sure, but rad anyway) meticulously arranged in special wooden desk shelves. All are monogrammed, all in her signature colors, brown and pink, and all from the most expensive stationers in the city, like Mrs. John L. Strong, Smythson, and Tiffany. So chic-adelic.

"Hey, amigo," said Whitney, who was plopped on her bed, reading the latest issue of *People*. She sat up and looked at me. "The

Bradley boys called. They want to hang as soon as possible. I told them that we were, like, busy with the St. Peter's boys tonight but maybe next week. I want to play hard to get with Jake."

"Good idea," I said, sitting on the bench. Bradley and St. Peter's were the boys school equivalents of Tate, and our Bradley guy group was made up of Max, Josh, Bobby—and Jake Watkins. There was ST (sexual tension) and little flirtfests here and there, but so far, it was nothing heavy—except for Kaitlin, who seemed to have hit it off with Max. Every year it seemed one school or the other had hotter guys, and this year it was all about Bradley, so we had to tread carefully. We didn't want them to go for the Briar girls (our rival school).

"Oh my gosh, your closet totally rivals Hilary Duff's!" said Sophie, emerging from Whitney's walk-in extravaganza. "Hey, Laura, I didn't even know you were here!"

"I just got here," I said, surprised. I had thought Whit and I would have some early hangout time alone. "I didn't know you were here either."

"Ava and Kaitlin will be here in an hour. They're still getting manis," said Whitney.

"Listen, I'm starvatious! What kind of grub do you have?" asked Sophie.

"Let's hit the kitchen and check it out," said Whitney.

Fifteen minutes later we were plopped in the kitchen, sitting under the hanging shiny copper pots, scooping raw Pillsbury cookie dough out of the weird sausagelike pack and scarfing on a giant bag of M&M's we had just acquired at D'Agostino's. Suddenly we heard the soft clacking of high heels across the pantry floor, and Whitney quickly pushed the cookie dough and candy in front of me. The pantry door swung open and Brooke Stanton Blake, Whitney's mother, entered.

"Girls," greeted Mrs. Blake, surveying the kitchen suspiciously.

"Hey, Mom," said Whitney, anxiously. Whitney was always nervous around her mom, which seemed kind of sad to me. Her mom wasn't that intimidating. She was like ninety pounds and had this ashy blond hair that she always wore in a black velvet headband. She looked pretty mild, in fact, but I know that she could be hard on Whit, who was stressed whenever she was around.

"What are you ladies up to?" asked Mrs. Blake. I saw her look at the cookie dough and candy and frown.

"Mom, this is our new friend, Sophie Mitchum. She's from L.A."

"Nice to meet you, Sophie," said Whit's mom, extending her bony arm, her gold bracelets jingling. "I'm Mrs. Blake."

"Nice to meet you, Mrs. Blake." Sophie smiled her best child-actress grin.

I could see Mrs. Blake's eyes dance down Sophie's body, taking in the explosion of designer logos all over her clothes (today it was Dolce & Gabbana) as well as her too-tight V-necked black sweater. She finally looked away and her gaze returned to the candy and cookie dough.

"What is this garbage you're eating?" asked Mrs. Blake.

"Oh, it's not mine," said Whitney quickly. "It's Laura's and Sophie's."

Thanks, Whit.

"I don't like this junk in my house," said Mrs. Blake sternly. She turned and looked at me, and I thought for a second she was going to bawl me out. "Hello, Laura, how was your summer?" she asked instead.

"Oh, great, thanks, Mrs. Blake. I was a camp counselor in Maine."

"That's lovely," she said distractedly. "Send my best to your parents."

"I will—" But before I could finish she turned to Whitney.

"Whitney, the preliminary sketches for your gown arrived. I'd like to go over them with you."

"Sure, Mom."

"Daddy and I are going to visit Peyton at Middlebury next weekend. I assume you don't want to come, so I'd like to discuss your plans."

"Oh, you can stay at my house!" interrupted Sophie. "We're doing a screening of my dad's new movie, *The Redcoats Are Coming*. It'll be an Oscar contender for sure."

"Cool, thanks, Sophie," said Whitney.

Mrs. Blake squinted at Sophie for a split second, and I could tell she was trying to figure what to make of this new buxom friend of her daughter's.

"That's very nice of you," she said, her manners finally taking over. "I'd love to meet your parents sometime."

"They'd be thrilled to have you for dinner. Their new chef is so good, he'll whip up anything you want. My mom is really into orange food these days, so it's, like, all on the menu. My mom's assistant, Taniqua, will call in advance to get your special dietary needs," said Sophie assuredly.

Mrs. Blake paused. "How wonderful. Well, I'm off to bridge," she said, and left the room.

Both Whitney and I sighed in relief when her mom left. I wasn't scared of her, but she was certainly chilly compared to my mellow parental units.

"Who's Peyton?" asked Sophie, sliding the candy bowl back in front of her.

"My NOTL brother, as in Nerd on the Loose," said Whitney.

"Is he at least hot?" asked Sophie.

"Barf!" said Whitney.

"Soph, do you have any sibs?" I asked. She had only mentioned her parents and her staff.

"Yeah! I have a half brother. He's forty-seven. My 'rents are like thirty years apart. So what's your *gown* for?"

"Oh, it's my Sweet Sixteen dress," said Whitney.

"Whitney's going to have the most amazing blowout. I can't wait," I said. "It's going to be at the Pierre. Gloria Vanderbilt is coming out of seclusion for it."

"You know, Sophie, you should think about having one. It's

the most important birthday," advised Whitney.

"You have to sign up with Ms. Hoffer, though," I said solemnly. "She's like a greasy hermaphrodite who was elevated from the gym department to keeper of the Book." Okay, so maybe we exaggerate a little, but she is pretty creepy.

"Her face is chipped Bryan Adams style from all the zits she picked. She gives me the cringe tingles." Whitney shuddered.

"Anyway, her sole job at Tate is making sure everyone's parties don't overlap, which is why she has The Book, which keeps track of everyone's party schedule," I explained.

"She couldn't be more bitter or diabolical," said Whitney.

"Gamy," I added.

"Malodorous." Whitney sniffed.

Sophie listened attentively as we continued our rant, making Ms. Hoffer sound like someone out of a Stephen King novel. Finally we paused.

"Oh, I already signed up with her for my rager," said Sophie proudly. "I found my way down to her dungeon—just followed the McDonald's waft. Gnarly, but worth it."

Both Whitney and I were surprised. Sophie certainly didn't waste any time figuring everything out. She only just got to Tate and she already knew about the Book?

"You're on the ball," said Whitney with a tight smile.

"Oh, I can't wait for my party. Donatella's doing my dress." Sophie beamed.

"When's your birthday?" I asked.

"January twenty-eighth," said Sophie.

Pin. Drop. Silence. I mean, crickets. This was major. My heart started racing. I could not believe this was happening.

After a pause so pregnant that septuplets could have been birthed, Whitney cleared her throat.

"That's *my* birthday," said Whitney finally.

"It is?" asked Sophie innocently. She scooped out a piece of cookie dough and put it in her mouth.

"Yes," grimaced Whitney.

"But the date was free in the book. Why didn't you sign up?" asked Sophie.

"I've been at Tate since kindergarten," said Whitney, tension mounting in her voice. "Everyone *knows* it's *my* date. It's like a known fact: The sun rises and sets, and Whitney Blake's birthday is January twenty-eighth."

"Well, the sun rises and sets in California, too, but nobody there knows it's your birthday," retorted Sophie.

"Are you mocking me?" asked Whitney angrily.

"No, but I don't think you have any right to be territorial about the twenty-eighth of January. You don't own that day. It's my birthday, too," said Sophie matter-of-factly.

I could tell Whitney was boiling, and it pissed her off even more that Sophie seemed so unfazed. But Sophie was right; it was her birthday also.

"Okay, you guys, no need for a thermonuclear meltdown," I said nervously. "We can find a solution without the U.N. peace-keeping envoy."

"Like what?" asked Sophie.

"Like . . ." I was trying desperately to buy time as Whitney and Sophie looked at me with eye daggers. "You could . . . have the party together!" I blurted out.

Whitney was about to say something, but I stopped her with a wave of my hand. "Before you respond, think about it for one minute. I'll time you."

I looked at my watch and held up my finger. I could see them both contemplating my idea, the way the contestants on *Jeopardy!* try to ponder their final answers. When the time was up, I motioned to Whitney.

"I don't know what my mom would think about that," said Whitney.

"Well, it's *your* party, not hers," I said.

"I don't know," said Sophie. "We've already ordered the favors—gold-leaf playing cards with my monogram and birthday engraved on them."

"Think about it, though," I said. "I mean, with your New York connections, Whit, and your Hollywood connections, Soph, it would be a legendary joining of forces. It'd go down in history like Truman Capote's Black and White Ball."

"Hmmm . . . you do have a point," said Sophie. "God, Laura, you should be like a studio head or something. You're so good at handling people."

"I know, Laura's like Kofi Annan. Scary. I don't know. I mean, it could be great," said Whitney. "But . . ."

"Look, why don't you guys take a week and think about it.

You don't have to decide now," I offered. "Ava and Kaitlin are coming over. Let's just hang out and have fun."

"Deal," said Whitney.

"Okay," said Sophie.

And so they started to think about it. I was proud of myself for arranging the temporary truce. But the more I thought about it, the more I kind of panicked. Was it actually a good idea? I was thinking on my feet suggesting that they have the party together. I just didn't want a fight. But maybe it wasn't such a great idea. I mean, one of them could have her party the weekend before; why did I need to suggest having it together? But if I knew Whitney, it didn't really matter anyway, because they would never have the party together. There was just no way.

Chapter Seven

I was totally astonished on Sunday when Whitney and Sophie conference-called me and said they had decided to join parties. I just never thought it would actually happen. I felt a twinge of jealousy and skepticism. Were they going to be best friends and totally ditch me? Just as I was doing an internal freak-out, they totally assuaged my fears. Whitney said directly that as her best friend I was going to be in full best-friend party-planner mode. I think she wanted to make it clear to Sophie and me that I was still number one in her eyes. And then Sophie praised me to no end for being such a great peacekeeper and encouraging them to work together. My ego was semi-stroked, so I decided to be positive: I would be kept in the loop as unofficial party planner, and both girls knew that they needed me as an unbiased supporter who would keep them in check. I pushed away my doubts and remembered that it was only a one-night thing. After January twenty-eighth everything else would be normal. Hey, if they were game, all the more power to them. With two enormous bank accounts and two determined fifteen-year-olds organizing it, it was bound to be a pretty sweet sixteen. Right?

Whitney and Sophie had each enlisted me to come along and help convince their moms that a joint bash could be great. A diplomat's work is never done. So the next day was a begfest.

Late Monday afternoon Sophie and I walked into the private room at David Barton Gym on 85th Street to see her mom mid-workout; Mrs. Mitchum's endorphins would be rushing, so Sophie figured she'd be happy and say yes. I almost fainted when I saw Mrs. Mitchum: She looked like a blond bombshell you'd see strolling BevHills, every muscle toned, tanned skin, jewels galore (even with her gym clothes), and slightly surgerized. Okay, more than slightly.

After brief introductions and downloading all of the reasons why a joint party was crucial to Sophie's social status, we awaited an answer.

"So what do you think, Mom?" asked Sophie. "It could be pretty cool merging Rolodexes!"

Mrs. Mitchum had been harnessed by her Russian bodybuilder personal trainer into her gyrotonics apparatus.

"I don't know, honey," her mom said, hanging from her ankles.

"Mom! It's *my* birthday!" Sophie protested. "I want to do it with Whitney. She's awesome, and it'll be such a major event if we join parties!"

"Excuse me," Mrs. Mitchum replied sternly from a flying lotus position, spotted by Sergei. "We don't have to join with anyone to be major. Your father's last three movies grossed a billion dollars total. They might just want us to foot the bill."

"Mother," Sophie said calmly, "that is so not the case. They are loaded, too. They have a Sargent."

"We have five Monets!" Mrs. Mitchum said. "Everyone knows 'old money' means '*no* money.' The higher the Roman numeral at the end of the father's name, the less dough."

I stood silently by. This woman was a real character; I saw where Sophie got her piss and vinegar.

"Then I'm going to ask Daddy." Sophie smiled as she dropped the D-bomb. Both of them knew that Marty Mitchum would give his baby girl anything her heart desired.

Mrs. Mitchum rolled her eyes. We knew it was a done deal.

An hour later I was over at the Blakes' as Whitney waged her campaign. "Pleeeease?" asked Whitney for the eighteenth time.

"Who are these people, anyway?" asked Mrs. Blake, looking at me. But before I could answer, she went on. "We know nothing about them. They could be ill-bred. Classless. Heathens. It could be a disaster!" Mrs. Blake continued, her tone horrified. "Those nouveau riche plebeians are generally nothing but Winnebago white trash," she pronounced. Sheesh.

"Mom, no!" Whitney protested. "They're really nice and they, they—" She looked at me, desperate for more alluring aspects to this family she hadn't actually met yet. Lightbulb. "They have this patisserie chef who will make whatever we want and do a nine-tier cake and everything!"

"Lovely," replied Mrs. Blake sarcastically. "Just what you need, more sweets. With those cookies you keep gobbling, we'll have to use the tent from your fifteenth birthday to fashion your gown."

Poor Whitney. She looked down, stricken. Her mom is such a bi-atch sometimes. But Whitney held strong. "Mom, we both have the same birthday. We're new friends. We want to do it together. My debutante ball is in just two years, and that will be all mine . . ."

Mrs. Blake looked off into the distance as if considering her daughter's sincere plea. And it was true, the planning of Whit's cotillion was only a year off. "If it's what you want, then I suppose—"

"*Thanks, Mom!*" Whitney exploded, overjoyed.

Victory! A successful allegiance had been formed, thanks to moi. Granted, I barely spoke at the plea meetings, but both Whit and Soph said I lent moral support. I was thrilled to have engineered a happy ending.

The next week brought passed notes with brainstorm lists of potential favors, color schemes, tablecloth materials, and music, all with my input, which was fun to give. Since they were eager to have another opinion on everything, I figured since I wasn't having a bash I could help with the fun parts of theirs—all the creative stuff and none of the stress! Or the bills.

After school we hit the newsstand and hoarded every mag, clipped pages of party looks from *Vogue*, and bought binders from Blacker and Kooby to start files on each aspect of the party. By Friday we were almost too wiped out for the movie premiere with the Mitchums. But Sophie nicely had her chef make us massive cappuccinos to go, which were sitting in the limo (still hot) when she picked us up at Whit's lobby.

"Hi, guys!" she exclaimed, decked out in a full-length Prada cranberry chiffon number. I was borrowing one of Whit's little black Chanel dresses while Whit was in head-to-toe Ralph Lauren. "Whitney, Laura, this is my mom and dad!"

"Hello, Mrs. Mitchum!" Whitney said.

"Nice to see you again, Mrs. Mitchum," I said.

"Ugh! Girls, puh-lease, call me Adriana. *Mrs. Mitchum* sounds like my dinosaur monster-in-law!"

Okay, weird slash refreshing. Mr. Mitchum looked quite a bit older but still very dashing. He was on his cell blasting some poor assistant pretty much the whole way to the theater, and he barely acknowledged us.

On the red carpet, I was almost knocked out by the crunch of camera peeps, but Whitney and I were in awe. Hundreds of cheering fans were held back by security and we were all waved through by the walkie-talkie people. Inside the grand, gilded cinema, Sophie seemed to know *everyone*. From the actors to the press people to the suits, she embraced them all, and with each hug or kiss she received, from Jack Nicholson ("Uncle Jack!") to Sofia Coppola ("So-Co!"), she always turned to us and introduced us formally, which was really nice and cool of her. Whitney and I kept exchanging thrilled glances; we were on a surreal high.

The whole thing put me in a daze. The movie rocked, but even more so because everyone involved in making it was hooting and cheering the whole way through, making it a mega–thrill ride. It was weird to be a part of that experience, but I was psyched that Sophie had included us. She had turned out to be truly cool, and I was so happy she'd become our friend. Life was getting interesting.

After a fabulous evening on Friday, Whitney and I went to lunch at Serendipity on Saturday. We always tried to go to lunch there every few months or so; it had been a ritual for us since we were little and our parents first let us go out to lunch alone. And because the first time we did it we had followed our frozen hot chocolates with a carriage ride in Central Park, we included that in our ritual also, rain or shine. We both knew it was terribly dorky, but we still had a blast. I didn't mention asking Sophie to join, and neither did Whitney. It's not that I wanted to exclude her, it's just that I didn't feel that I needed to include her in *every-thing* that I did, and I was glad Whitney felt the same way.

The day was truly fun, and mostly because we were goofy and silly and didn't talk about Sweet Sixteen parties at all. We made faces at the tourists that we passed in our horse and buggy and we blew kisses to the joggers. I was glad I had a little bit of Whitney back to myself, and it made all the birthday party weirdness temporarily fade to black.

That night, we reconned at the Mitchums' for our first fall Bradley Boy rendezvous, organized by Whit. It was pretty safe to say the Mitchums had just about the sickest pad I'd ever seen, including the ones on MTV *Cribs*.

"Whoa, Nelly," I said, wide-eyed, drinking in the lavish marble foyer with a double-height ceiling. It was very minimalist and modern, the antithesis of the Blakes' lavish chintz-filled abode.

"Come on up to my room," invited Sophie. "We've gotta change before the boys come over. Plus you guys have got to fill me in on the crew."

We walked up not one but two flights of stairs to Sophie's bedroom suite, which had its own private terrace. She had a giant pink princess canopy bed, and a framed signed picture from Leonardo DiCaprio hung on the wall.

"Okay, you guys, what do I wear?" Sophie said, sounding stressed as she opened the massive double doors to what I thought was the largest walk-in closet in New York. It was literally bigger than my parents' bedroom. "Laura, I am sooo jealous of your dress. I swear, your stuff is way better than Miuccia's!"

I looked down at my chocolate brown shift dress and smiled bashfully. "Thanks!"

"I have dibs on your next outfit, Laura," added Whitney.

Their compliments sounded crazy, considering they both had upward of a thou on their bods at that very moment, but it was still nice to hear.

The downstairs buzzer rang and Sophie grabbed the phone. "Oh, great, thank you," she said. "Kaitlin and Ava are here."

Our pals came up, marveling at the digs. "Worship this spread," said Ava, immediately checking out Sophie's handbag collection.

"Okay, you guys," Kaitlin said, gripping her cell phone. "Max just texted me and they'll be here in ten minutes!"

"Wait, wait, wait!" Sophie cried. "I need the bios again! I can't believe I am finally meeting the Bradley crew."

"Okay," began Whitney earnestly. "Josh is such a cutie. I've known him since we were zero. He's now madly in love with Laura, and so I am trying to work that."

"Oh, please," I responded. Josh was nice, but pas de sparks.

"What?" said Whitney. "He's a total catch!"

"Then you go for him," I responded, knowing full well she'd never go for someone like Josh—he was too insecure and not as hot as her string of boyfriends. It kind of bugged that she'd so eagerly pawn him off on me. That was one thing that nudged me about Whit. She, like, would stake out a man and then make me be the one to talk to him and strike up the friendship, then she'd snake him for herself and stick me with his best friend. This always happened when we were on vacation together. I mean, sometimes the best friend was cool and it worked out even better, but other times I was stuck with a total NOTL. But why was she trying to hook me up with Josh? Although he wasn't a total loser, she knew I didn't like him.

"That would be, like, incest! Our dads were roommates at HBS," Whitney responded.

"What, he's not cute, Laura?" asked Sophie.

"He's totally cute and nice, but there's no chemistry," I answered.

"He's a little insecure but he means well," said Whitney, looking in the mirror.

"Speaking of insecure," said Sophie, checking herself out as well, "I could not feel fatter right now. Greenpeace is going to harpoon my ass and drag me back to sea."

"Oh, Oprah's thinner than me," Kaitlin added, scoping her butt.

"I'm such a cow!" Ava said, chiming in. "I think I just heard myself moo."

"You guys!" I interrupted, annoyed. They were all drop-dead-gorgeous *sticks*. "You are all skeletons! It's so dumb and boring to talk weight. Next topic!" I said, silencing them. It was too yawnsville to waste time on thighs. It's the same old routine: One person complains they're fat, we all chime in on how fat we are, then we all tell one another how thin they are. Snooze.

"Okay," Sophie agreed. "Back to the boys."

"So," Whitney continued. "Max is Kaitlin's new macking partner—"

"Shut up!" squealed Kaitlin, turning hot pink.

"What?" said Whitney. "Don't pretend you haven't gone to third with him!"

"Whatever," Kaitlin replied sheepishly.

Kaitlin was, let's just say, very forward with the gentlemen. She was the first to go to first, the first to go to second, the first to go to third, and the first to do those other things that don't have bases to describe them. Like left-field, right-field stuff. She had no problem getting guys and was currently dating Max. Whitney tried to warn her that she could start to get a bad rep, but she didn't care.

"Bobby is a total babe," Whit continued. "And amazing at lacrosse. He wants to go pro. His coach says he has a chance. You'll really like him, Sophie. I've told him all about you. You should fully go for him."

I'd had a feeling Whitney would try to hook Sophie up with Bobby. He was definitely hot but also a total jock and hard to talk to about anything but sports. Not Whit's type at all.

"Perhaps," Sophie considered, smiling. "And what about that other guy . . . Jake?"

We all looked at Whitney, who took a deep breath. "Jake

Watkins. He is . . . gorge. And legendary. His mom is a Thurston, as in Thurston Industries—blood doesn't run bluer. They invented the brown paper bag as we know it."

"But he's more than just a stud horse with a stunning face," I added. He was not only hot but also the nicest guy ever. "He's kind of like a *New Yorker* cartoon—there's more than meets the eye with him."

Was I too gushing?

"Great analogy," Whitney said. "It's like he's sort of mysterious. He's fully besties with Bobby, Max, and Josh, but he also does his own thing. He and I totally hit it off this summer as well."

"Hot," said Sophie as the buzzer rang, announcing the arrival of the Bradley posse. "I can't wait to meet him."

And for some weird reason, I couldn't wait to see him.

Chapter Eight

Sophie opened the door and four very cute but very different prepsters stood on the threshold. Okay, full description: Max was kind of short, with gorgeous blue eyes, dark curly hair, and a prominent nose. He was the funny-guy type who would be the next-door neighbor on a sitcom and walk in and out making hilarious quips. It was amusing but sometimes did get a little tiresome with the chronic zingers. Bobby was tall and jocky, with blond hair and blue eyes—he looked like your all-American high school football star (maybe because he was wearing a varsity letter jacket). Josh was very thin and medium height, with sandy brown hair and brown eyes—kind of nondescript looking. He was super smart but a little defensive and kind of, I don't know, testy. Totally someone who will be a catch when he's, like, thirty and has some self-esteem, but not now.

Then there was Jake, the leader of the pack. He was tall, with brown hair and giant green eyes, and he totally knew how to dress. His features were perfect, almost pretty-boy perfect, and that could have been a total turnoff, except for one major redeeming quality: his teeth. The front one just slightly overlapped the other, and that minor imperfection is what made him so unique and beyond gorgeous. It's funny how one little flaw could make someone even more babe-a-licious.

"Hi, I'm Sophie," our hostess said, swinging open the door wide enough to let them in. Although not wide enough that they all didn't brush by her ever so slightly on their way.

"Soph, this is Bobby, Max, Josh, and Jake," said Whitney, pointing out the boys in a territorial manner.

"Sweet crib," said Bobby, waltzing in the door confidently and looking around.

Sophie brightened. "Thanks. Nothing compared to our house in L.A., but it's a roof."

"Cool art," said Max, pointing to the giant plain white canvas that hung on the front wall. "Except someone forgot to use paint!" He laughed.

"Max!" said Kaitlin in a singsongy voice.

"It's Kasimir Malevich, you idiot," murmured Jake.

Impressive.

"Sophie's fam has the most amazing art collection," added Ava, glancing at the boys nervously. She was always a little shy around guys. "Hello, MoMA!" she added with a hair flip.

Sophie ignored Ava's compliment and walked over to Jake.

"Wow, you really know your stuff—Jake, is it?" Sophie asked, cocking her head to the side.

Uh-oh.

"Yeah," Jake answered.

"How'd you know that? Do you have one?" continued Sophie. I could see Whitney watching this interaction very carefully.

"Nope," replied Jake. He walked over to the painting and looked at it closely.

"Hmmm . . . a man of few words," said Sophie, teasing. Okay, whoa. *Was Sophie flirting with Jake?* Hadn't Whit just gushed about him? Sophie was being pretty bold.

"Jake, don't you miss the Hamptons?" asked Whitney, walking over to him while twisting a lock of blond hair around her finger.

Looking at Whit and Sophie, I really saw how visually opposite they were. Both were all dressed up for the guys to come over, and for Whitney that meant putting on a new camel-colored Ralph Lauren cable-knit cashmere sweater, a long suede skirt with high chocolate brown Jimmy Choo boots, and her family heirloom diamond studs. But Sophie was all about short, tight, revealing, and logos.

"Nah. I was bored and ready to come back. How 'bout you?" he asked, turning to look at Whitney.

"Oh, yeah. I totally agree, I mean . . ." Whitney paused, trying to regroup and say something more, but obviously Jake didn't pick up on that, because he turned to me.

"Hey, Laura, what's up?" he asked.

"Not much, just hanging," I said. Lately when I was around Jake, I got a little tongue-tied. Which is so not moi.

"How was camp in Maine?" he asked. I was surprised he remembered.

"Good," I said. Okay, I was being a monosyllabic idiot. Bizarre.

"Hey, Laura," interrupted Josh. "I thought I saw you walking across the street last week."

"Really? Where?"

"Madison and Ninetieth," he said.

"Could be. That could be." I nodded, still watching Jake out of the corner of my eye. Josh bugged me, and I did not want Jake to think I liked him at all.

"Everybody, I ordered *vats* of Mr. Chow's takeout, so I hope you guys are hungry," said Sophie, walking toward the kitchen and taking control of the evening.

"Right on, minced squab with lettuce leaves. I'm all over that," said Josh, purposely walking next to me.

"Dude!" said Max, putting his arm around Kaitlin. "Give me some grub."

"You guys are pigs!" Kaitlin giggled.

"Hungry pigs," said Bobby.

After dinner, we all sprawled on the luxurious leather couches in the Mitchums' screening room to watch Ben Affleck's latest blockbuster. Dinner had been an interesting dance where we were all—except for Max and Kaitlin—trying to figure out if we were into one another, you know, on like, a romantic level. It was clear Whitney was way into Jake. And I actually think Ava was flirting (her feeble attempt at flirting, anyway) with Bobby. Despite Josh's clumsy attempts, I was categorically not into him. You can't be charitable when it comes to your heart. And although I felt bad, because he was so awkward and made all these stupid jokes, he was just so D.A.

But the crazy part was Sophie and Jake. She was clearly into him. I'm talking too-loud laughs, boobies-in-face, twinkly-eyed smiles his way. And Whitney noticed. And was clearly pissed. On the one hand I was like, *How dare she?* He's Whit's. But on the other, just because Whitney says something's hers, it doesn't mean it is. Let Jake decide. The thing is, I just knew he would never go for Sophie. He's not into flashy stuff.

On our way out of the kitchen, Whitney took me aside.

"What's the deal with Sophie? Admit she's, like, thrusting herself at Jake," she complained.

"Well . . . kind of," I replied.

"Do I have to spell it out for her that Jake is mine? Couldn't she tell from the way I described him? What the hell is her problem?"

"I think it's just in Sophie's nature to flirt. I mean, come on, she flirts with the guy in the deli, she flirts with the guy who plays the piano in chorus, she's just that way. I'm sure if you tell her later to back off, she will," I said. I hoped that was true, although I wasn't sure myself.

"You think so?" asked Whitney, twirling her hair.

"Yeah. I mean, come on, she's our *friend*."

"You're right, Laura," said Whitney. "Besides, Jake would never go for her," she said, walking down the hall. I sometimes wished I had some of Whitney's confidence.

The screening room had been pretty quiet during the movie, except for the disgusting macking sounds that Kaitlin and Max were making in the back row. Of course, Josh had pushed himself next to me the second I sat down—I even waited, pretending I couldn't decide where to sit so he would sit first—but he didn't bite and was totally rubbing up against me, too close for comfort. Luckily Jake was on my other side, next to Whit. It was annoying because Josh kept "accidentally" brushing into me when he reached down to grab some popcorn, and I would move away, which meant that I kept knocking into Jake.

Sophie's maid came in during an endless car-chase scene with a huge silver serving saucer of chocolate fondue and an elaborate exotic fruit tray for full-on dippage. Bobby, Max, and Kaitlin dove for it.

"Geez, Kaitlin and Max finally came up for air," said Josh.

Whitney leaned over. "They should get a room. Obviously didn't get enough affection as toddlers."

"It's all about zero to one, say the kiddie shrinks," I said. Jake flashed me a smile and I felt myself turn red.

"Now, now, you guys, let's let everyone else have some," said Sophie, carrying the fondue tray over in our direction. She leaned down toward Jake with the tray and totally thrust her boobs in his face. I saw Whitney grimace.

"Would you like some dessert, Jake?" Sophie asked. "It's Valrhona chocolate."

He stabbed a strawberry and dipped it in the fondue. "Thanks."

"If you want anything else, let me know. My chef will whip up whatever you want," said Sophie, lingering.

"Great, thanks," said Jake again.

Sophie wandered over to Ava and offered her some fondue while Josh again leaned in to me. "Isn't this a great flick, Laura?" he asked.

"It's all right." I mean, come on, it's a Ben Affleck movie.

"Yeah, sure, I mean, it's okay," said Josh, changing his tune. "I've seen better."

Okay, Josh, let's make up your mind and stick to it. Before I could respond, we heard a thud. We all whipped around and saw that Kaitlin and Max had rolled onto the floor.

"Wow," I said, laughing. "The hazards of PDA."

"So not my style," said Jake, turning to look at the fallen couple while shaking his head.

"Hellooooo, vomitorious!" Whitney whispered, giggling. "That's why God invented bedrooms."

Bobby leaned over to Sophie. "Speaking of which, want to give me a tour of yours?"

I could see Ava's face fall. Bobby was obviously not into her.

"Not really," said Sophie rudely.

Josh turned to me. "Laura, did you get Lilly McCracken's Sweet Sixteen invite? I almost barfed up my Lucky Charms when that messenger came to my door dressed as a headless horseman. What the hell was that all about?"

"'Cause it's held around Halloween, dude," said Jake.

"Ooh," said Josh, slowly getting it.

"I think it will be a blast; I'm really excited," Whitney said.

"So, Jake, are you going to the party?" asked Sophie.

"I guess," said Jake, noncommittal.

"You have to go!" interjected Whitney. "It's going to be amazing. I mean, not as amazing as my Sweet Sixteen—"

"*Our* Sweet Sixteen," interrupted Sophie.

"Right, the joint extravaganza that Sophie and I are throwing, but it will be a fine way to kick off the season," said Whitney.

"You guys are having a party together?" asked Josh.

"Yes," said Sophie proudly. "And let me tell you, there will be no contest once we premiere our blockbuster. All those other girls may think they know how to throw a party, but you're talking to the girl whose father screened his latest movie on a submarine hovering over the *Titanic.*"

"And my family practically hosted the first Thanksgiving with the pilgrims—we go *waaaay* back in the American party planning world," said Whitney.

Jake looked at them and smiled. He turned to me. "And are you involved with this?" he asked.

"Oh no," I said.

Jake leaned in closer. "Smart move," he whispered.

"I've been helping out a little with their rager, but mine is going to be more on the low-key side. Emphasis on low," I said, shrugging. "As in my parents and the gal posse going to a restaurant in the Village. Woo-hoo!" I hooted sarcastically.

"Laura is going to have a great party, just more intimate," said Whitney. "Girls' nights out are a blast!"

"That's cool, Laura—you can do a really fun night, even on your budget," said Josh.

Ouch. I could feel my face getting hot.

"What are you talking about?" asked Jake, throwing a pillow at him.

"What, dude? I just mean she doesn't have to drop millions to have a nice time," said Josh. I know he wasn't trying to be mean or anything, and it's not like I hid the fact that I wasn't a trust-fund baby, but I still felt a little mortified that he had to point out my family circumstances in a room full of people. In a private screening room in a penthouse triplex full of people, no less.

"Oh, my party definitely won't cost millions. No, no, no, the Finnegans certainly won't have Beluga caviar pouring out of Baccarat cups or talent jetting in from Vegas," I said quickly.

"Who cares?" asked Jake. "It'll be just as fun."

"Yeah," Josh jumped in. "Yours will be just as fun."

"It's going to be with my parents at some twenty-four-hour dive with fluorescent lights that do no justice to my pores," I said.

"Stop the drama!" moaned Whitney. "Chez Michel is hardly the greasy spoon you're bitching about. It's in *Zagat*."

"Whatever," I mumbled. "It won't be elaborate, just a mellow dinner. I don't even care; I just want it to be . . . memorable."

"And it will be," said Jake confidently.

Jake was so cool and always supportive. What a gem. Ugh, I had to stop myself from getting carried away. I couldn't like Jake that much. As far as Whit was concerned, the two of them were practically a done deal. Stealing the best friend's man (as if I could) was way lame. That's, like, a Paris Hilton move.

On Monday, after a seemingly endless day of classes (including a grueling pop quiz in French, which, thank God, I randomly knew the answers to), Sophie, Whitney, and I did a power walk down Fifth to the Pierre Hotel, site extraordinaire for the co-rager they would throw in just three months' time. I have seen many beautiful buildings in New York, but the painted rotunda of the tearoom took my breath away. We sat in a corner banquette, and while I drank in the gorge landscapes, Whit and Soph perused mags and whipped out the piles of potential linens.

"So here goes: I am so thinking toile for the tablecloths," announced Whitney.

"Oh my God," Sophie said, putting her hands to her face in shock. "Total ESP!"

"No way, you were thinking that too?" asked Whitney, laughing.

"Literally, Whit, I woke up last night and thought to myself: toile!"

A sea of businessmen entered while ladies sipped tea at a nearby table. I watched eurotrashy jet-setters blow by as the Mrs. John L. Strong, Dempsey & Carroll, Wren Press, and Cartier sample books filled our tabletop. When our three-tiered sandwich-and-scone platter arrived, the uniformed waiter wasn't quite sure where to place it but finally found a spot of glass among the heaps of sample cocktail napkins, napkin rings, place cards, even gold stirrers with different letters at the top. I dug in, popping bite-size sandwich triangles and buttery scones into my mouth.

"Call me crazy," said Sophie, nibbling the corner of a water-cress triangle. "I know this is kind of out there." She took a deep breath. "Zebra print somewhere. Just to mix it up." I raised my eyebrows but remained silent.

"Ooooh, I'm loving that," gushed Whitney. "A walk on the wild side."

"What's next on the agenda?" asked Sophie, perusing the pile of stuff that rivaled those on the desks of corporate lawyers on ten-year litigation cases.

"Okay," said Whitney, pulling out one of the massive files. "Here are the seven calligraphers auditioning for the job. We have to pick, like, today because the best ones get booked up."

"Total."

Sophie rifled through the different kits of sample fonts, ink colors, and ornate flourishes, the delicate strokes of the pens lovingly writing every letter of the alphabet for their approval. As I looked on curiously (I must admit, it was all over the top but fun nonetheless), Sophie must have felt bad for my third-wheelin' self (whose party stationer was the not-so-stylish Kinko's), so she asked how my birthday plans were going.

"Uh, just fine, I guess. I mean, there aren't really, you know, *plans*. My dad called and made a reservation. It's January fourth, FYI."

"Oh my God!" said Sophie suddenly. "I have the *best* idea!"

"What?" I asked. Maybe Sophie had thought of something cool to do after my birthday dinner.

Sophie cleared her throat dramatically and turned to Whitney. "Let's do individual birthday cakes for every guest!"

"Brilliant," said Whitney, nodding slowly as she pictured a thousand tiny perfect cakes in her mind's eye.

"And we can have them monogrammed in frosting with an interlocking S and W!" Sophie brainstormed aloud.

"Flawless," exclaimed Whitney. "This is literally gonna be the best party *ever*."

I was sure it would be. Then why was I so not revved up? The formerly delicious scones and sandwiches suddenly tasted sour; they felt like a lead weight in my stomach.

Over my mom's pasta surprise that night, I twirled my spaghetti into oblivion. I stared off into space with my forkful evolving into a gi-normous bite even a horse couldn't fit into its mouth.

"Laura?" my mom said. "Honey? Are you okay, sweetie?"

"Huh?" I said, broken out of my reverie. "Oh, sorry. I guess I was just—"

"Lost in thought?" my dad asked, grinning. He ate a big sauce-dunked bite of pasta he'd twirled in his spoon.

"Yeah." I didn't even want to get into what I was thinking about, but I felt terrible. Even though my parents so didn't get it in terms of what Tate was like for me, I also knew I'd rather have my parents—weirdo quirks 'n' all—over anyone else's at Tate.

"What's on your mind, honeypie?" Mom probed with a knowing look.

I exhaled.

"I just . . . ," I began. "I'm feeling a little strange about this whole Whitney and Sophie joint rager for some reason. I almost feel like I shouldn't have opened my big mouth suggesting they join forces. I mean, now they've merged, and I feel so dumb saying this but . . ." I could barely admit it. "I feel like the third Brontë sister."

"Charlotte and Emily's successes were mostly posthumous, but that's beside the point," my dad said, propping his glasses up on the bridge of his nose. "I think, my dear, that you did the right thing. You prevented conflict with a clever solution."

"I guess . . ." I shrugged.

"It seems to me," observed Mom, "that Whitney and Sophie have very different sensibilities. How do you think that will manifest?"

"I smell a Trotsky and Lenin debacle," mused my dad.

Finished with my food, I got up from the table and walked exactly three feet to my bedroom and perched at my corner sewing station, which looked out at the dining table. Buster followed me and curled into a ball on my bed. I pulled a bolt of black chiffon out from under the small desk and began to work on my newest dress. I was going to add velvet ribbon piping at the end, but I started with the sleeves. My parents watched me curiously, waiting for my answer. That was my parents: They never asked rhetorical questions; they always truly wanted to know what you thought, and they knew that sewing helped me sort out those thoughts.

"The thing is, they are both hard-core money-honeys," I responded, watching my perfect row of stitches. "I'm sure they will totally bond ringing up the cash register together."

I knotted off my thread. It gave me such satisfaction to make something. Some people jog ten miles to let out the day's aggression, some box a punching bag—I sew.

"This all seems like quite a production for a party," my mom said.

"Well, it *is* Sweet Sixteen," I said, cutting more fabric for the bodice of the dress. "It's a really important birthday. At least at my school. In fact, this dress I'm making is for yet another million-dollar Sweet Sixteen blowout." I turned the sleeve inside out to admire my craftwork. Perfection.

"Think of how much good you could do with a million dollars," fantasized my dad.

"Laura," my mom said while clearing the rest of the plates. "I wonder how sixteen got to be such a big-deal year. Do you know why it's such a pinnacle?"

"I don't know, Mom." I sighed with irritation. "I just know every girl wants to feel special on her sixteenth birthday."

Yes, I love that they analyze everything, but come on, do they really not get it? Sweet Sixteen is *major*. I hated that on my SS I was going to feel like Miss Mediocrity. And while it was great making clothes that I knew were cool, I was also annoyed that I *had* to make my clothes. Sometimes keeping up with the Joneses was overwhelming. Just once it would be nice to slip into my own Prada or Marc Jacobs frock. Just once it would be nice not to think twice about money. And although I could dissect and probe everything with my parents, and I knew on an intellectual level why things were the way they were, sometimes I just wanted to buy into all that superficial stuff. I mean, I'm in high school, for chrissakes. Isn't that what it's all about?

Chapter Ten

When Whitney and Sophie got wind that Cynthia Tedesky had rented out the entire Cooper-Hewitt, National Design Museum for her Sweet Sixteen, the kid gloves came off and the party planning spun into full gear. No one, I mean *no one*, was going to outdo their birthday bash. When they heard that Leslie Porter from St. Agatha's was giving everyone small silver Tiffany jewelry boxes (cuff link boxes for boys), they ordered *gold* jewelry boxes from Cartier. When Marjorie Landcaster sent out her invitation engraved in gold-flecked icing on giant Godiva chocolate bars, Soph and Whit ordered Save the Date cards from Vosges Haut Chocolat, encased in Swarovsky edible crystals. They seemed to have a whole team of rapid-response hacks working for them; it was like a political campaign—when they heard of someone else doing something original or interesting, they immediately organized a better, more expensive version. It was starting to border on insanity.

Besides the sheer wasted extravagance of it all was the gnawing unfortunate fact that—and I know this is so lame and immature—I was feeling very left out. Whitney, who'd been my B.F. since we were practically fetuses, was now glued at the hip to Sophie. I couldn't help but think, Who is this girl who just waltzes into our school and becomes Miss Popularity and steals my best friend? But Sophie wasn't really to blame. She was fun and exciting; who wouldn't gravitate toward her? And it had been my idea, much as I hated to admit it. Plus, Sophie always seemed to bend over backward to make me feel included by asking my opinion; in fact, she brought me into the creative fold even more than Whitney did! Whitney was the one who should have been a little more sensitive to my feelings. We had, I had thought, a unique friendship.

One day in science lab, Whitney, Sophie, and I were all sitting in a row while our teacher Mr. Rosenberg droned on and on about the *Lumbricus terrestris* (i.e., the earthworm). Mr. Rosenberg is one of those really intense, scary teachers. His class is way advanced, to the point where we would be dissecting a human cadaver at the end of the year, so he doesn't mess around. We'd have scientific-term spelling bees where you were literally disgraced if you couldn't spell *deoxyribonucleic acid* on cue. You had to listen to everything he said or else he'd humiliate you by "canceling your experiment" (i.e., dumping your pig carcass into the trash and giving you an F on the dissection). Practically every day he had someone in tears, and when he was really pissed he'd make you stay for hours in his creepy lab, which reeked of formaldehyde, until he was ready to reprimand you. Then he would lead you into his overgrown greenhouse, where scratchy plants gnawed at your clothes, and bawl you out.

In the midst of our class, Sophie slid a note to Whitney. I glanced at it out of the corner of my eye. It read: *I'm worried: Are 2,000 mini–Polaroid cameras enough?* Whitney paused and rested her chin on the eraser of her pencil, which she does when she is really thinking. She then scribbled back: *Let's make it 2,500 to be safe*. The second she slid it across the table, Mr. Rosenberg sprung into action.

"Sophie? Whitney? Is there something you'd like to share with the class?"

"No, Mr. Rosenberg," said Sophie innocently.

Mr. Rosenberg walked over to Sophie and Whitney and confiscated the notes. He held them up and read them aloud.

"What's this about?" he said angrily.

Whitney shrunk in her chair. She knew what she was up against. But Sophie was still new, so she had no idea.

"It's about our Sweet Sixteen party. Sorry, Mr. R., it's just something that was on my mind and I didn't want to forget it. But don't worry, I was totally listening," said Sophie, smiling her child-star smile.

Oh my, that girl has guts.

"If you're more concerned with the minutiae of your Sweet Sixteen party than the upcoming dissection, I foresee a cold and shallow life for you both," Mr. Rosenberg said.

Even Sophie seemed to be stunned into silence with that. Mr. Rosenberg continued. "Maybe it's time for you to climb on the reality wagon bound for earth." With that, he opened the three rings of their binders and shook out all of their papers into the garbage. Sophie and Whitney stared, their mouths hanging open in shock.

After that I totally thought that Sophie and Whitney might now take pause and really prioritize their life. I mean, getting on Mr. R.'s bad side was *major*.

But when I returned to the science lab after my last period to pick them up (they had been forced to sit there for the rest of the day), I found them unfazed.

"Hey, guys," I said, entering the room nervously. They were both on their knees, digging their notes out of the gore. After cleaning all of the animals' cages and watering every little fern in the place, they had finally been released. But Sophie and Whitney barely acknowledged me.

"Re: party favors," said Sophie, "do you think the Tiffany

initial necklaces for the gift bags, or those gold bangles for the girls?"

"The necklaces are sweet. But I also saw some awesome Bulgari gold bangles with semiprecious stones that are even better," said Whitney.

"Um, so, are you guys done yet?" I interrupted. I mean, hello, what am I, Casper?

"Oh, you go ahead, Laura. We have to discuss flatware and stuff," said Whitney.

I was pissed. How could they be so nonchalant? "You guys, is your reaction meter broken? Don't you care at all that you just got railed on by Mr. R.?"

"I'm fourth-generation Tate. My dad's on the board and he can get Mr. R. canned faster than you can say deoxyribonucleic acid," said Whitney smugly.

"But he could totally decimate your GPA," I insisted.

"Grade shmade. Laura, you're the brainiac who gets straight A's and will have the Ivys rolling out the red carpet. Even if I worked my ass off, I still won't do as well, so who cares?" said Whitney.

"And my dad just donated the Film Center to USC, and I'm in on a silver platter even if I'm hopeless in school," said Sophie confidently.

"You guys totally underestimate yourselves, but whatever," I said, turning to leave. They obviously didn't need me around to talk about flatware.

"Laura!" said Sophie.

I turned back. "Yeah?"

"We'll see you tonight? Operation San Gennaro?" asked Sophie.

"Yeah, sure."

"Did you get a chance to call Jake? Is he in?" asked Whitney.

"I left a message and then I missed his call," I replied.

"Could you call him again?" asked Whitney in her sweetest voice, cocking her head to the side. "Please?"

"Why can't you call him?" I asked, an annoyed tone creeping into my voice. Why couldn't she do her own dirty work?

Whitney looked surprised. "I don't know . . . I guess, you're just so much better on the phone than I am. I get all awky around him since we're, like, in the throes of early romance. I know, I'm lame, but just this once?"

"Fine," I agreed. I mean, it's weird that Whitney wants to, like, hook up with Jake and she only communicates with him through me, but fine. I don't mind calling Jake. Actually, the few times we have chatted recently, when I called on Whitney's behalf or he called me, we had really nice talks. I really felt comfortable with him, and our conversations flowed with no awkward pauses or anything.

"Thanks," said Whitney.

"What shall I wear to a carnival? I've never been to San Gennaro," said Sophie. "Is Prada too fancy?"

"Yeah, the festival is pretty grimy," said Whitney.

"Oh, too bad, 'cause I was going to suggest, Laura, that you wear that new lace dress you made. You look so awesome in it," said Sophie.

"Thanks," I said.

"Really, Laura, remind me to call Calvin Klein. He's a dear friend of my mom's. I totally want to link you two up. You could design for him one day," said Sophie.

"Laura's going to be a major designer," added Whitney.

"Thanks. Gotta go. See you later," I said, leaving. For some reason, suddenly their gushing compliments felt kind of condescending. Like they were trying to make me feel better about not having Prada in my closet or Calvin on speed dial.

I knew Sophie and Whitney genuinely believed I was a good designer, but I kind of felt like they were just being *nice* so I wouldn't feel left out. And quite frankly, I didn't want to succeed in the design world through their connections and introductions.

When I left school that day I had a really bad taste in my mouth. I had become a tagalong, and I didn't like it. I wouldn't even go to San Gennaro if it was just going to be the three of us, because I had had enough of Sophie and Whitney today. But I was psyched to hang with Jake. Just as a friend, I mean. After the pit in my stomach from the afternoon, a friend is what I really needed.

Chapter Eleven

When I got to the San Gennaro festival, I drank in all the flickering red, green, and white twinkling lights. Whitney, Sophie, Kaitlin, and I gathered at the appointed spot in front of the Ferris wheel and waited for the guys. Ava had been too scared to sneak out; her parents are so strict, she would have needed a whole Tom Cruise *Mission: Impossible* harness to pull it off, Quantico style. Lucky for me, I didn't even have to tiptoe or lie, I just told my parents I was heading out. But I knew everyone else didn't have it that easy. I just hoped the guys wouldn't get pinched making their respective exits. I still hadn't been able to get ahold of Jake that afternoon, but I'd left a message telling him where to meet us.

After a few minutes, we could see Jake, Bobby, and Max making their way through the crowd in our direction. For some reason I felt my heart skip a beat when I saw them. I tried to tell myself it must have just been the pure adrenaline of being out late at night in such an exciting environment. But when I saw Jake, who looked so handsome in his dark blue peacoat and too-long chinos, I felt myself flush. He had such good style—preppy but with a tiny bit of edge—and probably because I was so interested in fashion, I always took note of how well he dressed. Instead of buying into that lame "I wanna be a rapper" look that every other guy thought was so cool, he went for a casual, almost retro vibe, where everything he wore looked just thrown on and not thought out, like layered long- and short-sleeve tees, Polo pants, cute sweaters. What I liked about it was that it wasn't cookie cutter. He always had his own take on things. I realized I was looking too closely at Jake, who had given me a wide smile as he approached (with those cute crooked teeth!), so I turned away when the guys got closer.

Everyone in our posse enjoyed a group high-five with the boys for getting down unscathed, but before we could fully breathe easy, Jake's cell buzzed that he had a text message.

"Damn," he said, snapping it shut. "Josh was nabbed on the way out."

"Uh-oh. With his parents, he's headed on a Greyhound straight to Groundedville." Bobby laughed.

Sophie turned to me and touched my arm comfortingly. "Oh, Laura! Don't worry," she said. "Are you so bummed?"

"What?" I asked, weirded out. "No, not at all."

"Don't worry, we'll make sure you have fun without him," Whitney added.

I saw Jake looking at me and I suddenly felt ridiculous—clearly he now thought I liked Josh just because Whitney had decided I should. I had made it clear to both Sophie and Whitney that I was so not into Josh. Were they trying to embarrass me in front of Jake? That really made me mad. I mean, I get it, I get it, they wanted to make sure I had no designs on their man. But they didn't have to pawn me off on Josh to make their point.

"Yeah, Josh's parents are super strict," said Jake.

"My parents can't imagine why I'd go anywhere below Thirty-fourth Street, let alone a gross street party!" said Bobby.

"Parents are clueless!" Sophie laughed. "Mine still think I'm a virgin!"

Whooooa. Shock and awe. I looked at Whitney, who appeared floored. Even with all her hookups, she had not gone *there*. I mean, Kaitlin, the sluttiest of our gang, had just started talking about maybe giving it up to Max over the next summer. It was mildly awkward as we all stood there contemplating her random announcement.

“So you guys, let’s go get some food!” I offered to distract the gang, but of course Sophie’s bombshell gave a whole new meaning to the sausages that hung from every stall.

After gorging on endless eats, I suddenly felt extremely ill. I guess my face bespoke this as I turned a pale shade of green post–Tilt-a-Whirl, and Jake noticed.

“You okay, Finnegan?”

“Yeah,” I responded, sooo not okay. “I just feel a little food raped. I don’t think you’re supposed to mix meatballs and cotton candy. I feel dirty and violated inside.”

“Maybe this really fast circular motion ride will make you feel better,” he joked sarcastically, gesturing to the line we were on. “If you want, I’ll sit this one out with you.”

“No, no, no,” I protested. “This is my favorite one. I love the spinny stuff. I’m doing it.”

Our group approached the spinning teacups and I climbed aboard.

“I can’t go,” said Whitney, backing away. “I think I’m going to be sick.”

“Me too, I’m not doing that death trap,” added Sophie.

But I was already in the teacup, and Jake climbed in right next to me.

Max and Kaitlin broke tonsil hockey. “Hey—we wanna come!” she squealed.

“That’s it!” the ride operator said, putting his hand out to stop them from getting in our teacup. “And we’re off!”

"So long, wimps!" Jake taunted as we took off flying through the air.

"Oops, sorry, guys!" I called. As we lifted off, I felt weird being with just Jake, but I saw Whitney and Sophie pointing at booths below, so I knew they were entrenched in their rager research.

We flew higher and faster, and I saw Jake's eyes close.

"Are you okay?" I yelled.

"Yeah," he responded, bracing himself. "The centripetal force takes a minute for me to get used to." He opened his green eyes and smiled.

"Don't worry. The worst thing that can happen is our pod breaks off and goes flying into that cannoli stand, crushing a Sicilian widow."

"Thanks!" He looked at me and winked as we both screamed in unison with an outward spin.

A few minutes later, we got off the ride so dizzy that we looked like drunken sailors. Everyone was teasing us, laughing at our nerdy staggers.

"I feel nauseous," I said.

"Oh my God," Sophie said. "We had a totally brilliant brainstorm while you guys were on the ride!"

"Guess what we're gonna do," said Whitney. "We decided to just rent all the booths and have a mini–San Gennaro festival during the hors d'oeuvres in the first ballroom!"

"It's gonna be *beyond*," said Sophie, ecstatic.

"Cool," I said, gripping my tummy.

"Come on, Sophie," said Whitney. "We have to investigate. I want to hire some of these authentic people to come and man the booths. Let's go!"

Okay, ew. It was one thing for Whitney and Sophie to blow their party up into a huge drama, but it was another to actually cast these carnies for fun—or decoration—for their tableaux. Between them, the chow, and the rides, I'd had enough.

I looked at my watch. "You guys, I'm so sorry, but I think I'm gonna have to peel off—"

"Laura!" Sophie said in a singsongy voice. "Bummer!"

"Sweetie, it's okay, you go home to bed," Whitney said, kissing me good night. "We'll put you in a cab."

"It's okay, Finnegan, I'll take you home," Jake said. "I'm going to hit the hay too."

Whitney and Sophie were visibly shocked slash let down by his departure.

"What do you mean?" Sophie asked Jake. "It's still, like, so early!"

"Yeah," said Whitney, twirling her hair. "I mean, there's still two more blocks of festival."

"Hey, it's a school night, gimme a break," Jake said, zipping his Patagonia jacket.

"You only live once," said Sophie with a flirty tone. "You can sleep when you're dead."

"Then I'd be a zombie while I'm alive," he said. "I'll catch you later."

I could see Whitney bite her lip. She wasn't sure what to do. She sure as hell didn't want Jake to leave, but she would never be forward about it. Sophie also looked upset that Jake was leaving, but I could see her relief that he was leaving with me and not Whitney.

Max and Kaitlin broke from their kiss. "Wait—Jake," Max said, "we were just saying we should all hit Bowlmor Lanes on Saturday night."

"Yeah, they have a great DJ spinning," said Bobby.

"Sounds fab!" said Sophie, looking at Jake as Whitney watched. "Should we say seven?"

"Fierce," said Jake, and turned to hail a lone cab down the block. "C'mon, Finnegan!" He took my hand and practically yanked me down the street into the taxi.

"Phew," he said, turning to me once we were inside. "I'm glad you wanted to bail. I don't know how I am going to get up in the morning. I have a soccer match on Randall's before school. I am clearly toast."

"I have to dissect a frog first period," I remembered aloud. "That funnel cake is gonna be mid-esophagus."

He smiled. "Classic Finnegan line."

"What do you mean?" I blushed. Damn pale cheeks. Was he complimenting me or making fun? He just smiled.

"So what's up with Sophie?" he asked with a slyly raised brow.

"She's really something, isn't she?"

I felt myself deflate. So that was it. He wasn't into *Whitney*, he was into *Sophie.* He clearly thought she was a hottie. I mean, who wouldn't? She's a blond stick with knockers.

"Sophie's awesome," I said honestly. "She's so nice and really generous and a burst of energy all the time."

"She really speaks her mind."

"Yeah, I admire her balls-out directness. We really needed someone like that at Tate." I felt semi-bad for building up Sophie when Whitney liked him, but hey, it was the truth. And even though I was fed up with them both today, they were still awesome.

"It's strange," said Jake, looking at the tree-lined twisting streets of Greenwich Village. "She and Whitney are such opposites. But you're right, they're both really fun girls."

"Yeah," I agreed, now trying to figure out which "really fun girl" he liked more. They both were full-on knockouts in their own way; Whit was a Ralph Lauren ad come to life, and Sophie was more of a Britney-esque saucy firecracker. As I was contemplating Jake's choices, I saw him look at my dress, which had an Edwardian lace collar and a billowy knife-pleat skirt, all in ivory, with a black grosgrain ribbon I'd used as a makeshift bow belt.

"That's a cool outfit, Finnegan."

"Oh, thanks," I said, looking down. "I made it myself."

"Oh yeah, ha ha."

"No, I really did."

"You did?"

Uh-oh, did he think that was so loserish? "I know it's sort of dorky, making my own clothes. It's my hobby, I guess." I looked out my window.

"It's not dorky, I think it's really cool. You're an original."

"Thanks," I said, buzzing from the compliment. "My dad brought back this fabric for me from a conference in Jaipur."

"That's so thoughtful," he said, staring out the window. "I doubt my parents even think of me when they're away."

"Do they travel a lot?" I asked, trying to keep pity out of my voice.

"All the time." He paused. "So do you think Sophie is into Bobby? He really digs her." Okay, abrupt change o' subject. I guessed since he kept asking about Sophie, Whitney was not at the forefront of his mind.

"Um . . . Bobby? I don't think so."

"Oh. So, are you and J—?"

Just then I noticed the cab speed by my house. "Oh! It's right there! I can get out here, sir!" We screeched to a halt and I opened the door. "Thanks, Jake. You're awesome to get me home and make sure I'm not, like, hacked to pieces."

"I'll wait 'til you're in the door in case the serial killer strikes."

"Okay, thanks!" I got out and waved. "Good luck with your game tomorrow!"

I slammed the cab door and ran to our house. As I hopped up

the stairs and scavenged my keys from my bag, I turned to signal safe entry and saw Jake give a salute from the rear window before the taxi pulled away. There was a fluttering sensation in my gut, as if I had swallowed a pigeon whole. Oh boy, I thought to myself. *Jake is really perfect in every single way.* "Shut up, Laura, shut up, Laura."

Chapter Twelve

Maybe it was the giant green formaldehyde frog splayed across my tray, dissecting pins holding down his skin so that I had a good view of his guts. Or maybe it was residual Tilt-a-Whirl motion sickness. Perhaps it was too many calzones. I didn't even want to consider that my upset stomach had anything to do with Jake. But I spent most of the next morning running in and out of science class to barf my guts out in the bathroom. I didn't want to totally bail on the dissection because it was fifty percent of my grade, and Mr. R. was such a stickler about finishing the whole process, but after my seventh trip he finally took pity on me and let me out of his carcass-filled lab to go rest in the lounge.

I was also semi–freaking out on another level, because Sophie and Whitney were no-shows at school. I had been calling them all day (between trips to the bathroom) and kept getting their voice mails. Neither Kaitlin nor Ava had heard from them, and we all agreed that it was totally weird. (Annoyingly, Ava, ever the goodie-goodie, was now gloating that she didn't go to San Gennaro. She said I got sick and assumed Whit and Soph were no-shows because they'd gotten in trouble for staying out late, so what good was it? I think she was just jealous that she was too chicken.) Anyway, this was so not like them to be total MIAs.

After trying yet again to reach my amigos on the pay phone (my parents still wouldn't cough up the dough for a cell), I finally lay down on a chaise in the lounge with a makeshift compress (aka wet paper towels) stuck to my forehead in an attempt to assuage my nausea. My eyes were closed and I was about to drift off when a beefy hand tapped me on the shoulder. Barf. It was Ms. Hoffer, clad in her trademark purple velour sweatsuit, with a giant number eleven emblazoned on her chest.

"How is a scholarship student able to afford renting out Chez whatever for a Sweet Sixteen party?" the Kmart lover gruffly asked.

I was stunned. What? "I . . ." I didn't know how to continue. First off, everyone *knows* I'm on scholarship; I don't try to hide it, but it's not so polite or necessary to broadcast it in the lounge.

"What, cat got your tongue?" she demanded.

"I'm not renting it out. I'm only having six people to my party." I sat up and took the paper towels off my head. Did I really need this now?

"Oh," she said, running her hand through her greasy hair. "Listen, Laura," she began, and sat down next to me, I mean, right next to me, so that I could smell her Kentucky Fried breath. "I really sympathize with you. I know it isn't easy being around all these ungrateful richies, is it?"

"Um . . ."

"I see them. I see these princesses prancing around the halls and out into their chauffeur-driven cars. I listen to their stupid squawking. They think they're so great, but let me tell you something: They piss and crap just like the rest of us."

I guess *flabbergasted* would be the only word to describe how I felt. "Um . . ."

"It's hard for you," said the Beast, putting her hand on my shoulder. "I know. It's been hard for me, too. So if you ever need to talk to someone, you can speak openly to me. I'm on your team."

She looked at me, waiting for a response, but all I could do was gulp. *I am* so *not on your team.*

"Thanks . . . ," I mustered.

Ms. Hoffer stood up and looked at me. "You know, Laura, you and I are a lot alike."

When she turned to walk away, the music from *Psycho* screeched in my brain, interrupted only by the *swish swish swish* rhythm that her pants made. A lot alike? Please, God, nooooo!

After my little Hoffer interaction, I decided to call it a day. Whatever temporary stomach bug I picked up at the festival was still ravaging my bod, and there was really no use in sticking around with Soph and Whit gonzo. Besides, I only had art left. The subway ride home didn't help my condition, so when I finally got to my pad I beelined for my bedroom and crashed. My parents decided not to wake me for dinner, and I ended up taking the biggest power nap of my life and sleeping until 9:30. Fun Friday night. When I got up, Sophie and Whitney still hadn't called, and when I tried them, I still got their voice mail. I couldn't figure it out. Had they mentioned they were going somewhere? Was it something to do with their party? It was odd, but I just ended up eating a bowl of strawberry ice cream and watching *Law & Order* reruns until I fell asleep.

I had been planning to hit Chinatown on Saturday morning for a day of sleuthing around the fabric and textile stores for inspiration. This was something I did monthly, and I always preferred to do it alone. I actually never even told Whitney when I was going because I didn't want her to tag along. Nothing against Whit, I just liked the solo reconnaissance missions, and when I had distractions I couldn't really concentrate on my creative impulses. So I woke up early, ate my raisin bran, and bid adieu to my parents, who were already knee deep in grading midterms.

"So they never called?" asked my mom before I left.

"No, and I'm kind of worried. It's so odd; they've never disappeared like that," I said, putting an apple in my knapsack.

"Maybe they caught the flu as well," offered my father.

"I hope not. That bug was awful. But please just tell them if they call that I've gone to Chinatown to scout some fabrics and I'm worried about them. And tell them to leave a number where I can reach them."

"We'll relay the message," said my mom.

"Thanks, guys."

I had a great day walking around looking in all the tiny shops and surveying the wares of various vendors. I loved that you could find anything in Chinatown, from little plastic slippers to neat little purses. It was all borderline tack but also could be very chic. And they marked this stuff up to high heaven in department stores, which was so hilarious, because if those women who bought it even ventured downtown they could save so much dough.

Throughout the day I tried Whit and Soph from various pay phones where I probably contracted hepatitis D, but I was concerned. There was still no answer. By now I was oscillating between panic and sheer irritation. I mean, if something happened, I would be beside myself. I shuddered. But on the other hand, what if they were okay and they were doing something together, maybe something fun, and they hadn't bothered to call? That would be more than lame. I would really be irate. But I couldn't imagine they'd be that evil. They were probably just grounded and their parents took away their phone privileges. That was a surefire way to make them repent.

When I got home there were still no messages. We were supposed to meet up at Bowlmor at 7:00, and I knew that Sophie and Whit would move hell or high water to hang out with Jake, so I figured I'd go anyway. It was only a few blocks from my house (one of the few attractions that would draw my Upper East Side friends down to the "scary" Village), and I had nothing to do anyway.

When I got to the bowling alley there were tons of people—groups of teenagers, some ten-year-olds having a party, and beer-swilling twentysomethings all hitting the alleys. But no Sophie and Whitney, and no guys. I looked at my watch. It hadn't stopped, had it? It said 7:00. I knew I was crazy about being on time and most people weren't like me, so I sat down and decided to wait.

For a while I sat next to this very lovey-dovey couple in their early twenties who kept pawing at each other. It had to be the early stages of their relationship, because no one can sustain that kind of interest forever. I mean, the guy helped the girl put her bowling socks on. Gross. It would be kind of neat, though, to feel that excited about someone. I really couldn't imagine; I had never been in love. There was a guy that I "hung out with" at camp, and yes, we kissed twice, but he was definitely more into me than I was into him, if I do say so myself. It was also a location relationship, because I would never go for him here. Thank God he was from Boston.

As the clock ticked by and it got later and later, I started to get annoyed. I used the pay phone to call Soph and Whit and then Kaitlin and Ava, and even my parents, and there was no update from anyone. I decided to wait until 8:00, and when no one showed, I walked home. It was a crisp autumn night, with the leaves crinkling under my shoes as I walked past all the stores on my way. I loved this time of year in New York. There was something about the way the light fell across the city that really illuminated the true beauty of Manhattan. Summer was disquishously too hot and humid here, winter was far too cold and snowy, and spring was okay but it really only lasted for a nanosecond. New York was all about fall. It was just so romantic. I really wished that I had someone to share it with. At that moment, aside from being annoyed with Whit or Soph, I thought of Jake. It's not illegal to dream.

Chapter Thirteen

After a Sunday split between studying and worrying about Sophie and Whitney, the dread buzzer sounded: my Monday-morning alarm clock. After I hauled my carcass out of bed and onto the 5 train, I noticed I had a few minutes and enough change to splurge on a double espresso to get my brain working. I walked past Tate up to Yura Café, home of three-buck muffins and four-smack mochaccinos, where yummy mummies and their perfectly preened tots waited in a snaking line for warm *pains au chocolat* and freshly squeezed juices. Through the giant, recently Windexed vitrine, I was stunned to see Whitney and Sophie holding mugs and sharing a croissant. As I pulled the door open I had a wave of hurt slash fear slash anger; it was like when you're running down the stairs and you skip a step and think you're gonna fall splat into an X. It was a stomach-pit feeling like that.

I entered and just stared, as if after a gazillion stalkerish voice mails they were just ghosts in front of me.

"You guys?" I asked, clearly in wounded-deer mode.

"Laura!" Sophie squealed, getting up to give me a hug. "How art thou?"

"Where the hell have you guys been?" I demanded, looking mostly at Whitney.

"I'm so sorry, Laura," my supposed best friend replied. "I heard all your messages after we got in late last night. I didn't want to wake your fam and you don't have a cell, so—"

"What?" Now the limping Bambi was gone and I was a full-on writhing lioness. "I have been beside myself freaking out! Back from where?"

"It was totally sponty," said Sophie. "We took Friday off to go to Holland to look at flowers for the party."

"You *what*?" I was too stunned to even blink. "You *flew* to Europe?"

"Yeah," Whitney added. "It really was spur of the moment."

"You could have told me. I was worried sick. Literally."

"Sophie's father was shooting a film there and they had the

jet, like, fueled and ready, it was so quick," Whitney said.

"Oh, and I suppose there was only room for two where you stayed," I said sarcastically. But Whitney and Sophie clearly didn't understand sarcasm.

"Oh no, we stayed in this amazing villa," said Whitney.

"And we looove the hybrid Dutch tulips we found! This nice farmer dude is gonna grow them custom!"

A feather could have knocked my ass over. Holland? For flowers? I couldn't bring myself to exhale I was so wound up. "Leaving a two-second message would have been nice," I said angrily.

"Come on, don't be mad," Whitney said.

"I'm sorry, Laura! We so didn't mean to exclude you," said Sophie, giving me a hug. I looked over her shoulder at Whitney, who was casually picking up her book bag, looking like she didn't have a hint of real remorse.

"Whatever, I'm over it," I lied. I was so pissed I almost burst a blood vessel. But I didn't want them to see me sweat. "I have to go. We're going to be late for homeroom."

I walked briskly back to school, and Sophie started running to keep up with me. I could tell she felt bad.

"Don't be mad, Laura. We really didn't want to offend you. It was all so last minute," she said imploringly.

I continued walking and wondered why it was Sophie who was making all the make-up effort and not Whitney. In fact, Whitney was taking her sweet time walking behind us and blowing on her latte so that it would cool down.

"Oh! Laura," Sophie said, opening up her Michael Kors satchel. "We brought you back a present."

"Thanks, guys. But I can't, like, be bought off with gifts. It still was majorly uncool of you to do that to me."

"Come on," said Sophie, grabbing my arm so that I would stop walking. "We so are not trying to 'buy you off,'" she said with finger quotes. "We were at the Van Gogh Museum, and we just know you love Vinnie Van G."

"You're going to love this," said Whitney, catching up to us. "Come on, forgive me?" she asked, batting her lashes as if to say *Pretty please?*

I didn't say anything.

"You're right, we suck, but we still want to be your best friend," pleaded Sophie.

"And we love you to death. Please forgive us," added Whitney.

I sighed. I was really pissed off, but what could I do? I could just continue pouting, but there was really no point. With all this party stuff it was like aliens had seized Whitney's and Sophie's brains and allowed them to think of nothing else. They were being totally exclusive, totally inconsiderate, and totally lame, but I could only hope that when these parties were over they would return to their human selves. I promised myself to be more wary of them, to keep more of a distance, but ultimately I had to move on for now.

I opened the box to find a book of paintings along with a key chain of a plastic ear. Okay, I had to grin. "They weren't selling these severed ears at the museum, were they?"

"No." Whitney laughed. "That part was from the street vendor outside. How hilar?"

"Very." I smiled, but slightly. It was nice to bring a gift, but I wasn't totally letting my guard down just yet.

That night over dinner my parents saw I was being very quiet. I was having a movie montage in my head of flashes of Sophie and Whitney's bonding—shopping at Club Monaco, getting manicures at Trevi Nails, planning the rager. I knew my third-wheel status had shifted into high gear.

"Threesomes are very tricky," my dad said. "Allegiances shift constantly. But trust me, it will blow over."

"I know I have no right to assume I could jet to Europe at the drop of a hat. I just feel . . . very left out. Ugh, this is so third grade of me! I am pathetic."

"No, you're not!" said my mom, putting her arm around me. "This is human nature. And Dad's right. It will all pass."

"Meanwhile," said my dad, changing the subject. "Honey, tell Laura about those little disposable Polaroid cameras you found!"

"Oh, yes! We found these wonderful little cameras for your Sweet Sixteen! They make these tiny instant pictures!"

"Sophie and Whitney are having, like, more than two thousand of those at their party," I said.

"Two thousand cameras?" said my mom, incredulous. "I'd hate to organize *that* photo album."

"I'm sure they're hiring a staff to do it for them. They're hardly sitting there with glue sticks." I put down my fork. "You guys, I am so sick of these parties. I don't even want one anymore."

"Why wouldn't you want a party?" my dad asked, his voice filled with concern.

"We'll get the table in the window. It'll be great," said my mom, trying to get me excited.

"I feel like everyone's staging these huge crazy elaborate events. What's the point of my even having one when no one will remember it?"

"Honey," my dad said, leaning in. "Do you make memories for yourself or for others?"

"Dad, I really don't want a lecture."

"Extravagant scenery and luxuriance do not make for more colorful recollections," my mom added.

"Maybe not in your world, but in my world they do."

"Are we orbiting in such different worlds, Laura?" my dad asked.

I felt the blood rising up in my veins. "All my friends get everything their hearts desire! Every shiny new watch, every beautiful dress on Madison Avenue—"

"Your clothes are much more beautiful, honey," my mom said.

"You have a unique style," my dad added.

"I am tired of making all my own clothes."

"But you always look stunning!" my dad said.

"It doesn't matter! Listen. You knew the lion's den you were sending me into when you enrolled me at Tate. You had to know that keeping up with the Joneses would be impossible. And guess what? It is!" I felt tears burning their way to my retinas as I retreated to my room. I hated being an ingrate and making my parents feel bad, but I also hated being some pitiful scholarship case the gym teacher bonds with over being poor. A little while later I heard the phone ring. "Oh, yes, one moment, she's just in her room."

My dad popped his head in the door.

"Laura—"

"Is it Whitney? Tell her I'm busy."

"No, sweetheart, it's Jake."

His name was a sudden balm on my emotionally weary bones. "Okay, thanks, Dad."

I picked up and weirdly got nervy. "Jake?"

"Hey, Finnegan." Geez, his voice was hot.

"How are you?"

"Oh, just okay. Crazy day at school, blah blah blah." Why could he make even the most mundane blabber sound sexy? "So, Finnegan"—why was I oddly obsessed with the way he said my last name? I mean, so asexual and stuff, but hot nevertheless—"why was the whole Bowlmor shindig called off? I got the message from Whitney and Sophie like an hour before."

What? They called Jake from Holland to neg and still didn't even call me? I felt all the color drain from my face. I couldn't believe it. They made it sound like it was impossible to get to a long-distance phone line and yet they had easily found one to get to their object of affection. I gulped and put on a fake chipper voice. "Well, you're lucky you got any heads-up! I was kicking it solo with all these pins falling around my loner ass."

"No one called you to say it was canceled?" He sounded surprised. "Lame. I called Max and Bobby, but I figured you of all people already knew. What was their reason, anyway? They said they were out of town."

"Yeah. Just ever so slightly 'out of town.' Try over the border, across the ocean."

"What?"

"Yup. Holland. *Europe*. The continent."

"No."

"They didn't tell me; they just disappeared, milk carton style." Just thinking about it made my blood boil.

"Dude, that sucks. And of course you were probably stressing that they went AWOL."

"Coronary. I thought they were fully incarcerated post–San Gennaro and were doing time for sneaking out. Little did I know they were selecting custom hybrids for their Sweet Sixteen centerpieces."

"Listen, I know you guys get all jazzed up about this birthday crap, but who cares?"

"I don't know, it's just, like . . . the thing people are obsessed with this year. Mine's totally going to be lame, but whatevs."

"Don't sweat it, Finnegan. I'm sure it'll be a blast."

"We shall see."

"Speaking of which, are you going to Lilly McCracken's party on Friday?" he asked.

"Yes, I'll be there. I heard she's having giant chili peppers on stilts and fire-eaters."

"Well, she is the hot sauce heiress," he said, laughing.

"Isn't it so funny they make gazillions off one product that makes people's tongues burn off?"

"Absolutely. It's all crazy. You are one of the few sane ones."

The pigeon was in my tummy again. What did he mean by that? "Well, I'll see you at the hot sauce rager then."

"Sleep tight, Finnegan."

Ah, there it was again—my last name sounded so . . . sexy coming out of his mouth. But I couldn't let myself be lulled into Jake fantasies. I had a mission. I picked up the phone and called Whitney and totally launched into her when she answered.

"I can't believe you called Jake from Holland and didn't call me. Really, Whitney, besides the fact that you totally hurt my feelings, you also lied to me, excluded me, ditched me, and were completely lame. I am really disgusted by your behavior," I said, pausing for a second to get my breath.

I could tell I had caught Whitney off guard and she had no

idea what to say. "It's not like that, Laura . . . ," she began defensively. Lovely, I couldn't wait to hear this. But suddenly she switched gears. "You're right. It was so lame of me, and Sophie, but more lame of me because I am your best friend. I really have no excuse."

I wasn't expecting that, but I didn't want to let her off the hook. "So, what, I, like, don't even merit a phone call in your eyes?" I asked angrily.

"You do, you totally do," she said quietly. "I don't know, Laura, I guess I just got really swept up in this whole offer of Sophie's to go to Europe, and I've been totally obsessing about my party and I guess I've gotten a little competitive with her. I didn't want her to go to Holland without me, and I knew we had to decide quickly, and then I didn't want to blow it with Jake so that she could snake in there, because let's face it, she's going to go after him. And I know I could have e-mailed or called you, but it just got so busy so fast, and I'm sorry."

I paused. I knew Whitney was being sincere, but I couldn't help but think that the abyss between us was widening a little. Pre-Sophie, Whitney would never have done this. And even though she admitted to being "swept up" in everything, if she was aware of that, why didn't she try to avoid doing it?

"Okay, whatever, I'm tired and we'll talk tomorrow," I said, suddenly exhausted and unable to think about this anymore.

"Okay, see you tomorrow," she said.

When we hung up I sat on the edge of my bed stroking

Buster's tummy. What we had done right now was merely put a Band-Aid on our friendship, just a temporary patch that would not help the wound to heal. In fact, our relationship was starting to cry out for surgery.

Chapter Fourteen

I had residual hurt feelings about my whole Laura-in-the-dust paranoia, but I decided to shove my anger under the antique oriental, pretend all was peachy, and try to have a good time. I arrived at Whitney's house, where Sophie, Ava, Kaitlin, and I had all arranged to get ready for Lilly's shindig. Second only to Piper Sorenson's Dead Presidents bash that summer in the U.S. Mint building (her great-great-great-grandfather invented the way money is printed as we know it) and Electra Firestein's Denim 'n' Diamonds party (her family controlled the biggest blue jeans production factory in the world, which sold their fabric to, like, every designer in the Barneys jeans bar), Lilly's party was poised to be the blowout of the year. So far, at least. A limo was waiting outside, and Sophie's mom's soap-star friend's makeup artist was over to do our faces. I actually opted out—I always felt too self-conscious and drag queen–ish when I wore makeup. I went au naturel except for a little self-applied smoky gray eye shadow and sheer lip gloss.

As Whitney was lying back getting her face dabbed with a powder puff in her mom's room, the rest of us were zipping up our gowns and angling for viewage in the three-way mirror.

"I am clinically obese," moaned a stick-thin Kaitlin. "Max is going to FedEx my ass to Jenny Craig."

"I am a full-on heifer," bitched Ava. "Somebody please brand and filet my ass and send me to Lobel's Butcher Shop. I am enormissima!"

"Oh no, here it goes, the nightly cellulite squeeze. You guys, please can it! You are stunning!" I protested.

"Come on, Laura, we can't all be naturally as svelte and fashion savvy and chic sans makeup as you are," said Kaitlin, putting on even more mascara. "You're like so easy low maintenance. Some of us have to work at it, yo."

"Oh, please."

"You look sooo great, Laura," said Sophie, glancing at me.

"Thanks, Sophie. I love your dress."

"Listen," she said, her voice lowering so Ava and Kaitlin

couldn't hear. "Can I talk to you for a sec?"

"Sure." I followed her into Whitney's dressing room.

"Laura, I want you to know I am just eaten up about the whole Amsterdam field trip. I feel terrible."

I tensed now that the subject had been brought up, but then exhaled; I was glad she was feeling remorse.

Sophie looked to the doorway and continued in a whisper. "I feel awful because I *knew* we should have phoned you. I asked Whitney if we could call and invite you to come with us and she said not to."

"What?" I felt a crossbow hit my gut.

"She said you're not into glitzy stuff like that and that it should just be the two of us. I feel heinous and evil, and I just want you to know I would never come in the middle of you guys. You were so invited and always will be. It'll never happen again."

I looked into Sophie's blue eyes and knew she was telling the upsetting truth. Somewhere deep down in my marrow I knew Whitney had been distancing herself from my un-glam self. Clearly my lack of a private jet and famous friends and fancy parents was not as alluring as the company she'd been keeping with the Mitchums. And it broke my heart.

"It's okay, Sophie," I said, my voice almost cracking. I was touched by her honesty. I gave her a hug and we went back in the bedroom, but I was nervous to see Whitney now that I knew she'd tried to keep me out of their new dynamic duo.

Whitney soon made her grand entrance—she had

maneuvered it to get her makeup done last so it was the freshest—and she did look beautiful. But I felt ill watching her preen so cockily.

"I think tonight's the night, girls," she pronounced, flipping her hair in front of a Venetian mirror.

"For what?" Sophie asked.

"I think I'll finally lock lips with Jake," Whitney said mischievously, purposefully not looking at Sophie.

The second punch in the stomach of the evening. My heart started racing. Although I knew, of course, this moment was bound to happen, I suddenly couldn't bear the thought of Whitney and Jake together.

"I am so kind of scoping out Bobby," said Ava. "Is he too male slut, though?"

"Hellooo," said Kaitlin. "Ava, he's laid more pipe than Con Edison. Total player."

Funny, Kaitlin was always the one to call out other people's sexual activity, even though she was more active than the rest of us.

"We should go, you guys," I said. "It's, like, past fashionably late." At this point, after finding out about the betrayal of my best friend and that she was moments from macking with Jake, I just wanted to get the whole eve over with.

As the limo pulled up to the *Intrepid*, we saw fireworks exploding overhead on the water. The Hudson River rippled with the cold wind, and the lights from a half-mill display of fireworks lit up the night sky and water below. On board, the name LILLY was spelled out in lightbulbs that flashed in concert with the DJ's music on a turntable sound system that rivaled any major club's. Waiters on Razor scooters came by with mini-hot-sauce-infused pizzas while jugglers, fire-eaters, dancers, performance artists, and caricaturists lined the decks.

We checked out the main deck and then decided to troll the scene first before choosing a place to plop.

"Oh my God," said Sophie. "Our centerpieces are gonna kick Lilly's centerpieces' ass!"

"Totally," said Whitney, scanning the room for Jake. "We've cruised all three decks; I mean, dónde está the guy?" Whitney pushed an errant hair back behind her ear. "These gusts are killing my 'do. Laura, can you go get the guys? Bring them back here, and we'll get bevs."

"Fine." I sighed. I was not in the mood to be fetcher girl, but I was more than ready to get away from Whitney. Dispatched by her majesty to alert the boys of Whitney's presence, i.e., sausage run, I took my time to ponder my situation. I don't know why it bummed me out so much that Whitney planned on hooking up with Jake. I guess because I saw how quickly she caught and dropped boys. She'd wash her hands of him before next week's manicure. Plus the discovery that she'd sold me out made me even less tolerant of her calculating ways.

"Hey, Finnegan."

I turned around. Jolt to the aorta. Jake looked positively James Bondian. So dashing I thought I might fall overboard. "Hi—"

"Is that one of your designs?" he said, nodding at my outfit, a crimson organza strapless dress I had sketched while watching an Audrey Hepburn movie.

"Yeah." I blushed, then remembered my critical mission. "So, um, we're all hanging out on the other end of the boat, on, like, the stern. Or the bow? Down there," I said, pointing with my whole arm, Vanna White style.

"Cool."

"Do you guys want to come down there? Where's your posse?"

"Probably in the bathroom doing shots out of Bobby's flask. Josh is there with them."

I was so annoyed Whit and Sophie had planted this dumb Josh seed—argh! "Oh, well, whatever. Why aren't you with them?"

"Don't tell anyone, but I am a little seasick."

"I'm so sorry! Can I get you anything? Ginger ale?"

"No, no, it's okay. I always feel like this on boats. Kind of lame when we're not even cruising."

"Don't worry," I said, feeling his pain. "I fully tossed my tacos the day after our little Tilt-a-Whirl odyssey."

"No way!"

"Yeah, just a tad too much spinning and spaghetti."

"There you are!" Whitney suddenly appeared and kissed Jake hello. Sophie followed closely behind. Ava and Kaitlin were nowhere in sight. "Laura, we thought you were man overboard."

Just then the guys came back from the bathroom, minus Max.

"Dude, I am hammered," said Bobby, leaning on Jake in an exaggerated drunken manner.

"Yeah, we, like, had so many shots," said Josh, trying to impress the crowd. "Max is fully praying to the porcelain altar."

Nice.

"This boat is now fully rockin'!" Bobby laughed. He was truly so immature. Such a meathead, too. Why is the jock cliché never a cliché?

"Hey, Laura, 'sup?" asked Josh, turning toward me with a slightly tipsy look. "Wanna go dance? They flew in these DJs from Berlin, so fierce."

"Maybe in a little while," I said.

"Killer necklace," Josh continued, touching my Cartier chain.

"Yeah, it's sweet," said Jake.

"Um, yeah, I . . . actually borrowed it from Whitney."

"Yes, it's Cartier," said Whitney, jumping in. Usually she never made a big deal about lending me stuff, but I guess since Jake admired it, she wanted him to be sure he knew it was hers.

"So," said Jake, turning to Sophie and Whitney. "You two taking notes for your big party?"

"As *if* we would have such cheesy bar mitzvah–esque décor," sniffed Sophie. "I mean, name in bulbs? No grazie."

"Dorkus Maximus," pronounced Whitney, surveying the scene. "And this whole nautical theme should be on the ocean floor with the anchor. Please, do they think they're old-line Newport?"

"Um, waiter? Can we have a vat of Meow Mix sent over here?" Jake mocked.

"Feline fighting!" cried Josh. "That's better than WWE."

Bobby and Josh started making catcalls.

"Oh, Jake, we're just being bitchy!" said Whitney, suddenly laughing off her oh-so-serious comments as jokes. "So, are you going out to Southampton for Thanksgiving?"

"Yeah," said Jake. "I'll be out there."

"Cool. Let's go to the movies one night," said Whitney, tilting her head to the side flirtatiously.

"I haven't been to a movie theater in, like, ten years," said Sophie, leaning back seductively, showing her killer bod in her too-tight-for-my-taste dress. "I mean, premieres don't count. Jake, you should fully come watch flicks in my screening room!"

Whitney clearly looked taken aback by this invitation and the boob shot that accompanied it. I sensed Whit's tension level ratchet up a notch with Sophie's bold move. Good—it wouldn't kill her not to automatically get what she wants for once.

"That sounds awesome!" said Bobby, clearly not getting that the invitation wasn't for him.

"Or we can just be mellow and hang out at my house," offered Whitney. "I want to chill this year. We can raid my parents' Scotch vault like last time," she said coyly.

"Oh, we can always drink at my house; my parents are cool like that. We're from L.A. It's a lot more relaxed there," said Sophie.

Whitney's eyes became daggers. I could see the rage mounting in her face. Great, all we needed was a real catfight. Much as I hated to get involved, it was time to break it up.

"You guys," I said, trying to break the budding tension in the night air. "I'm like *starvatious*! I think I just heard my stomach literally growl. Serengeti style. Let's peruse the buffet."

"I'll meet you there," said Jake. "I'm going to go find Max and make sure he's not still booting."

"Laura, want to do some shots?" asked Josh, offering me his flask.

"No, thanks. I'll catch you later."

Josh and Bobby went off after Jake, and Whitney, Sophie, and I stood there in silence. Except for the blaring Moby.

"Sophie, what the *hell* was that?" Whitney asked with a piercing tone.

"What are you talking about?"

Uh-oh. Meow.

"You were totally throwing yourself at Jake!" replied Whitney, seething.

"So?"

Wow, pretty bold of Sophie.

"*So?* It was embarrassing."

"Why was it embarrassing? 'Cause I took his attention away from you?"

"You guys—" I tried to intervene, but to no avail.

"Jake is *mine*, Sophie!"

"I think he would be pretty surprised to hear that he is *yours*," snapped Sophie.

I took a step backward so I didn't get smacked by the ricochets of their meltdown. This was getting interesting, and they clearly weren't listening to me, so I gave up trying to defuse the situation.

"What is that supposed to mean?" asked Whitney.

"You do the math, Whitney," Sophie said. "He's not interested."

"Are you insane? You don't even know him, you bitch!"

"You think you are so great. Clearly Jake doesn't agree."

Oh. My. God.

Whitney's face was the shade of the chèvre-stuffed beets going by on a Segway.

"You. Tacky. Pathetic. Los Angeles new-money *namedropper*! While you were getting melanomas in Malibu, Jake Watkins and I were sneaking into Marquee! Your manipulations may work on the coast, but you are *nothing* here."

"Interesting," replied Sophie coolly. "I always knew you were a Waspy repressed virgin, but I didn't realize you were so competitive with me. You must have a complex. That's the problem with the *old money* you're so proud of. You're scared of the people who actually know how to make it."

"You trashy little upstart!" Whitney screamed at Sophie.

"You asexual joke!"

"Whoa, whoa, people—" I said desperately. This was *beyond* nasty. I had to do something. "Let's just calm—"

"To think I was going to share my Sweet Sixteen with such an unrefined, fake-tanned, low-class tart!" Whitney sniffed.

"You think you're such a princess. You act like you're forty!" Sophie laughed.

"You are *out*!" pronounced Whitney. "I am weeding the friendship garden!"

"I hope Mummykins and Daddykins arranged a marriage for you with some closeted, social register, trust-fund loser, because you'll never snag a guy yourself."

"Conversation terminated," said Whitney. If she'd had a scythe in her handbag, Sophie's head would have been lopped clean off. "Fasten your seat belt for a bumpy ride to hell."

"Ooooh, I'm so scared!" Sophie said, dripping venomous sarcasm. "Anyway, my party is going to kick your party's zombie ass!"

"We'll see about that."

Until tonight, I had believed the *Titanic* was the most horrific aquatic disaster. Boy, was I wrong. Shaken to the core, I flung open my front door and threw my clutch onto the couch dramatically. My parents, who had been totally engrossed in *Charlie Rose*, looked up with concern.

"What happened?" my dad asked, muting the TV.

I took a deep breath and fully downloaded the epic, bloody battle.

"I'm still reeling," I said breathlessly when I'd finished. "I've never seen two people be so nasty to each other. It was practically a bullfight, but they were both seeing red. I'm freaking out."

"Are you okay?" asked my mom. She put down her knitting and wrapped her arms around me. "It's upsetting to see unbridled rage like that."

"It was the most major fight *ever*. And now the joint Sweet Sixteen party is officially off—I mean, *off*." I pondered the enormity of what had gone down. "Can you *believe* this is happening? One day they're off to Europe, and the next they are at each other's throats over Jake!"

"Is that the young man who always calls you?" asked my dad. Leave it to him to take forever to understand the major importance of something.

"*Yes*, Daddy, but that's beside the point. They both like Jake, and now they are sworn enemies because of him," I said, picking up the stacks of periodicals that took over every surface of our overstuffed armchair, dropping them to the floor, and flopping myself down.

"That's too bad," said my mom.

"I'm not surprised," said my dad, scratching the stubble on his chin. He always did that when he was thinking long and hard about something. (Which means he did it every second.) "These girls are very different. They made a superficial bond, which is always tenuous."

"I just can't believe it. They were inseparable one second, and now . . ."

"If they're really friends, I'm sure this will all dissipate. In fact, I just read a UCLA study describing that whereas young men have a *fight and flight* propensity, young women always choose *tend and mend*. They generally make up because they are plagued when they are in a fight," said my dad.

"Oh, and you should read *You Just Don't Understand: Men and Women in Conversation*, sweetie. It's a brilliant analysis of—" began my mother before I interrupted her.

"You guys, I'm sure that's all great. But the thing is, this war was unlike anything you ever imagined. And lucky old me is caught right in the middle. I don't know what to do."

"Just be a good friend to both of them," said my mom.

"And stay above the fray," advised my dad. "It will all work itself out eventually."

I hoped so. That night when I was lying in bed I tried to imagine what it would be like if Sophie and Whitney *didn't* make up. Maybe it wouldn't be so bad, I thought for a second. I mean, they had started to get really exclusive and mean and totally dissed me. But on the other hand, they were both so strong-willed that it had the potential of getting really *nasty*. A chill factor on their instant-best-friendness might not be the worst thing in the world, but I shuddered to think what life would be like if they were sworn enemies. I had to take my dad's advice and just stay above the fray.

Chapter Sixteen

After a heart-pounding weekend of managing to avoid repeated phone calls from both camps by claiming illness (Whitney sent a basket from E.A.T. and Sophie had Aaron Carter leave me a voice mail wishing me to "get well soon"), I knew I had to face the music. My parents thought it was bizarre that I was playing Greta Garbo, but I just wanted to be mentally prepared, and I didn't want to say anything to either Whitney or Sophie over the phone that I would regret later. (It was convenient that they both turned to me when I'd previously been the spurned one.) It was better to deal with both in person and try and get this whole crazy chaos sorted out. But on Monday morning I had nowhere to hide, so I knew I had to face the mega-drama.

It was Community Service morning, and on top of having my two friends be sworn enemies, I had to haul ass to Harlem to the Union Settlement Soup Kitchen to feed the indigent. All these years I had actually enjoyed it and felt rewarded by the experience, but this time I was so wound up I could barely ladle. Luckily, Whitney didn't have Community Service this semester, so I would be solo with her archnemesis.

Sophie and I only had a second to chat at first, during which time she threw her arms around me and profusely proclaimed how thrilled she was that I was feeling better. Before I could respond, we were assigned to serve the two soups, and faster than the speed of light, the line of homeless peeps rounded the block, ready for their grub. We sprung into action.

"Carrot ginger bisque with fresh chives or winter squash with a dollop of truffle cream?" Sophie politely asked a man who was wearing a Hefty bag.

He grunted, surveying the two choices. "The orange one."

She handed it to him as I kept pouring out the bowls. Once we'd developed a rhythm and the line was moving, Sophie turned to me.

"Laura, we have to talk."

"Okay," I said, hoping this was a step toward peace.

"I really like you. I think you're awesome," she said. "And I know you have a history with Whitney, which I totally respect. But you and I became friends later in life, as adults; we weren't just thrust together in kindergarten. To me, that's more real."

"Look, Sophie," I said. "I think you guys are going through some momentary insanity with the other night, and I don't want to pick sides, and—"

"Wait, don't say anything," she said, interrupting me. "The thing is, I didn't want to tell you before, but when we were a triumvirate, Whitney walked all over you. You're, like, her lackey, and you don't need that crap. Plus, that whole Amsterdam trip? I told you, Whitney fully knocked my idea to have you come with us, same with when we got manicures and went shopping last week. She was trying to freeze you out. I mean, what kind of best friend is that?"

I felt ill. She'd struck a nerve. I thought I was going to barf. But I now had sandwiches to serve.

"Reggiano and pomodoro panini or prosciutto with minced fig?" I asked a guy with a beard longer than Santa's.

"Meat?"

I handed him the prosciutto and minced fig.

"Look, Sophie, I really can't deal with this right now. I know things have been crazy lately, but I think we can all gel again."

"Please," said Sophie, dashing that dream. "You really think a pocket full of doves are gonna come flying out and we'll all ride the peace train? Party's over. That loser is history, and *I know* that

you know she's a bad friend. As for you and me, we have a totally more real connection, and I hope you can see the light about her."

I served panini in silence.

"Come on, Laura, I think you rule—we're still friends, right?"

"Yes, of course—"

"Good," said Sophie. " 'Cause I really want you to come to my family's compound in Aspen over spring break; it'll be a blast."

After that Kaitlin came up and we couldn't talk any more. Throughout the day I could tell that Kaitlin and Sophie seemed to be tighter than ever, and Kaitlin seemed thrilled to have Sophie to herself sans Whit. Whitney was always a little judgmental about K's slutdom, whereas Sophie obviously didn't share Whitney's prudishness. I sighed. We were totally on our way to becoming a class full of Crips and Bloods.

Back at school I aced the history test I'd been jamming for all weekend to distract myself from the wreckage, and then I had to run down to art class, where I knew I'd see Whitney. We had a male "model" (who was hideous) posing buck naked for us to draw at our easels. As he reclined on a chaise with his fat rolls all over the place, I couldn't help but think that normally we'd be dying laughing at the skinned roadkill that was his chest hair, but the mood was too dire.

"I'm so glad it's just back to us." Whitney sighed, smiling at me. "Sophie totally insinuated herself into our clique. I'm thrilled we did a housecleaning."

I kept drawing the gargantuan thighs, and I could feel Whitney's eyes burning into me with her impatience for a comment. It could have been easy if I'd just agreed and returned to our twosome, but Sophie had been nothing but nice while Whitney had been sort of rude and exclusionary. If I teamed up with Whit, I would just be betraying myself—she was so quick to drop my ass and bond with Sophie, and now she wanted my solidarity.

"Whitney," I started nervously. "Until you guys patch, I think I'm just gonna be my own private Idaho—"

Wrong response.

"Laura! You just don't get it!" she snapped. "Wishy-washiness is so *lame*. Sophie is out and you're in! This is good for you. I mean, you never notice these things, but she really ignored you and tried to align herself with me and boot you out of the way."

"I don't know if that's true," I answered, drawing a beefy upper arm.

"I think it is." She stopped sketching and looked at me. "Anyway, on to better topics, I wanted to make sure you know you're invited to spring break with us to the Bahamas. It's gonna be amaaazing."

Before I could respond, Ava came up and Whitney gave me a look so that I wouldn't mention the invitation.

"Come on, you guys, let's go sign up for the French Club's party. It will be très très," said Ava.

"All right," said Whitney, wiping her hands. "You coming, Laura?"

"You guys go ahead. I'll see you later," I said.

I watched Ava link arms with Whitney as they wandered off. Ladies and gentlemen, add Ava Bisset to Whitney Blake's corner. The teams were dividing up nicely.

After art, I had math and then I stopped by the lounge to switch books in my closet. Sophie appeared next to me.

"Hey, Laura?"

"Hi, Sophie—"

"Sweetie, listen, I have a favor—after all that, like, craziness over the weekend, I'd love to get back on track with Jake. I really felt a big-time chemistry between us. I mean, not to brag, but he was fully checking me out and doing some rack-scopage at my house the night we met."

"Uh-huh—"

"So I was thinking maybe we could all hang out soon—can you call to invite him to my place? I'll screen the new Brad Pitt movie. You're the best!" she said, hugging me and flashing a huge smile without waiting for an answer. "Oh, and feel free to tell him a lot of guys have been calling me." She winked and left before I could protest.

After class I was in the same spot, getting my next book, when Whitney came up. "Laura! Listen, I need you to do me a massive favor. Can you call Jake tonight and just say how sorry we are that we all left so abruptly? I feel like there's weirdness now. Maybe we can chill this weekend and get some sushi?"

I suddenly felt sick and just wanted to pull the ejector seat.

"You know what, Whitney? No, you call him."

Whitney looked stricken. "Laura, please . . ."

"I really don't like being your phone service. You do your calls."

"You're right," she said. "I am so wimpy."

"You guys are friends," I said, surprised by her reaction, but determined to make my point. "So he'll be psyched if you call."

"You're right, Laura. As usual, you are right." I liked to hear her repeating that line. "Okay, but if I don't call him and you happen to call him or he calls you—and I know you will because you said you had to tell him about that MoMA exhibit, well, please just mention this weekend." She air-kissed me and was gone before I knew it.

Crap. She had put on the charm to get me to do her dirty work yet again.

I was starting to feel very used from both sides. But it was too early to call Sophie and Whitney on it. I knew if I said anything they would both get all wide-eyed and deny everything. And what could I say? "You want me to ask Jake over, and that's the only reason you're my friend?' I didn't believe that was exactly true, and right now I couldn't be totally sure their full-on Mary Poppins attitude toward me was a farce, so I decided to wait it out. I hoped that by the end of the week, everything would be glossed over and they'd be back on speaking terms so I wouldn't have to be the rope in this immature tug-of-war.

But, as the day crept on, there was more tension circling

Sophie and Whitney than ever. Mean looks, whispered insults, and harsh comments muttered a little too loudly were becoming common whenever we were all in the same room. The whole atmosphere was toxic.

I left school never more psyched to be free from the war zone that my life had become. I had just exhaled my first breath of relief when suddenly my body stiffened once more when I heard the spine-tingling word "Finnegan!"

It was Jake from across the street. I waved, still startled, as he zigzagged his way through Fifth Avenue traffic and approached me in full post-soccer mode. He was wearing his coat over his Bradley uniform, had an unknotted scarf across his neck, and his knapsack and gym bag were swung casually over his shoulder. He looked . . . really good.

"I've been yelling your name for the last three blocks, young lady. Haven't you heard me?" he asked, breaking into a wide grin.

"Sorry, I'm kind of in a daze."

"I see that," he teased. "You were like zombie girl." He did his best *Night of the Living Dead* impression, which normally would have been hysterical except I was so nauseous from the day's tension that I couldn't bring myself to break into a grin.

He looked at me, noticing I wasn't down with the whole pod people shtick.

"Laura, are you okay?" he asked, his cute brow furrowed and his voice laced with worry.

"I don't know," I lied. Truth time: "Not really."

"Why, you got an A minus on your algebra test?" he joked.

"No. Our class is, like, Yugoslavia right now."

"What happened?" he asked, cocking his head to the side. I'd noticed he does that when he's really listening to someone. Was it total betrayal to vent? Especially when he was the reason for the blowup? But he looked at me with such concern that I decided to fill him in.

"Whitney and Sophie had a major fight. I mean, epic. Kaitlin was totally glued to Sophie all day, and Ava is Velcro-ing to Whit. And little old me, well, I'm kind of stuck smack in the middle."

Jake thought for a moment before responding. "I thought you'd hang with Whitney; you guys have been friends forever."

"Yeah, but . . ." I paused. "I don't want to bore you with this petty stuff."

"No, tell me. Seriously."

"It's just that Whitney kind of ditched me when Sophie arrived and now she wants me back. I was the toy that got shelved for the glitzier new version, and now I've been rediscovered since the flashy toy's broken."

"Okay, wooden doll," he said, grinning.

I smiled. "I'm serious! I love Whitney, I do, I just feel like it's not that easy to simply shake the Etch A Sketch and make it like it was before."

"It was inevitable they'd have a meltdown," Jake said, shrugging. "Their friendship was shot out of a cannon. Plus, they're total opposites. You've got sassy Sophie from California and Princess Whitney from the Upper East Side. Oil and vinegar."

Hmmm . . . I wasn't sure what he meant by that. Was "sassy" a good thing? Or was "princess" a good thing? Maybe he just wanted to get off the topic so he wouldn't have to reveal which one he liked? Suddenly I felt awful downloading all this crap to Jake, who *they* liked. I tried to backpedal a little. "Maybe I'm being unfair. I mean, I really do love them both. Whitney is so generous and Soph's really fun and cool . . . I'm hoping this all blows over."

Jake gave me a knowing look. "Come, on, Finnegan. Not happening."

"Well, I can dream, can't I? They have good hearts, they really do. They're both awesome girls. And . . ." Should I mention the fight was about him? I mean, that's what they wanted, right, for him to know they had the hots for him? "They both really like you a lot," I finally added.

Jake didn't acknowledge what I said and looked away. Before I could subtly reintroduce the topic, he pointed to the fountains outside the Metropolitan Museum.

"Whoa! Look at that koi in there! Those things are huge!"

Jake gestured to an enormous shark-sized übergoldfish swimming in the Metropolitan fountains. We walked over to take a closer look.

"I have never seen anything that gargantuan," I mused. "I'm shocked that a Second Avenue sushi joint hasn't poached them yet. Where did those come from? They aren't usually here."

"I know, I go to the Met all the time and have never seen those." He looked up and pointed to a sign. "Ahh, see? It's for the Japanese garden exhibit. Good prop."

"Boy, they're huge."

"You should see the ones in Tokyo," Jake said. "Literally as big as a squash racket."

We kept strolling down Fifth Avenue; I'd already passed six bus stops. Oh well.

"Did you know goldfish only have a memory of twelve seconds?" I asked him.

"No way. Weird!"

"Imagine if you put one of those aquarium treasure chests in their bowl! The fish would be so psyched all the time, like *Oh my God, there's a treasure. . . . Oh my God, there's a treasure!*"

Jake looked at me in amazement before bursting into hysterical laughter. Obviously he liked my little goldfish impression.

"Laura, how the hell do you know all this stuff?"

"I'm a magnet for useless information."

"Like what else?"

"I don't know," I said, smiling. I looked at him, and he was grinning at me, waiting for an answer. Suddenly I felt this weird electric tension between us. He was so sweet and easy to talk to, I sometimes forgot how damn handsome he really was. I just loved his teeth—God, I loved them! Swept away in the moment, I seriously almost leaned in and kissed him. Or told him how much I worshiped him, and that he literally could make any moment better just by being there. Just as I was about to say something that would haunt me for the rest of my angst-filled teenage years, I came to my senses, thank God! How could I let myself get carried away?

First off, that would be so harsh to do to Whitney, who had announced at the beginning of the year that she wanted him. And Sophie was pretty obvious about making her intentions clear. How lame would it be if I was like "Me too! I want Jake!" I couldn't make things messier. And besides that, for all I knew, Jake was madly in love with either Sophie or Whitney. Then I'd really look like an idiot. No, no, no, I couldn't betray my friends like that, or risk saying something when I didn't know how Jake felt. Although deep down, the thing that bummed me out the most was that I knew Whitney and Sophie were not really, really into Jake. I mean, of course they liked him 'cause he's gorgeous and nice, but they didn't understand him the way *I* did. It was so irritating the way they both just jumped on bandwagons because things were cool. If only *I* had realized I liked Jake first. But as usual, I was the last to know, and now that I knew Jake was the most amazing person in the world, it was getting harder and harder to be a loyal friend. But I had to do it.

At that moment I was relieved to see my bus pull up to the stop. "Oh, there's my bus," I said hastily, and started to walk toward it.

Jake looked momentarily disoriented but recovered quickly.

“Brainstorm more fun facts,” he demanded, watching me climb aboard. “I’ll call you tonight; you better have one for me.”

The doors closed and I waved through the window as the bus pulled away and made it through the yellow light just as it was turning red. Luckily he couldn’t see that my face and heart were as red as the light.

Chapter Seventeen

There is always a quiet before a storm, and the next two weeks were just that. Although Sophie and Whitney were now sworn enemies, furiously recruiting classmates to their sides and planning their respective bashes with Martha Stewart–esque detail, they had accepted that I wanted no part of their campaigning and agreed to essentially back off. And even though I was called in by both Whit and Soph to confer on every little seemingly irrelevant thing, like what kind of flatware to have or if the waiters' uniforms should have gold or mother-of-pearl buttons, I was somehow able to navigate between the choppy H_2O remarkably easily. But the best news was that even though they talked practically every third second of every day about their parties, I did have some mellow hangage time with Sophie and Whit that was just fun and low-key sans party mentions, reminding me why I liked them.

For example, one day I took Sophie around NoLita and showed her all my favorite haunts, like the new Cath Kidston store, which had the most amazing retro British prints, or Jane Mayle's rocking clothing boutique that made every shirt seem like one of a kind. She was totally cool and into the whole scenario. In fact, Sophie was almost a different person below 14th Street, and she totally ditched the whole name-droppy and show-offy attitude that had sometimes bugged me. We had a long fun lunch at Café Habana and she fully fessed up Oprah style how insecure and nervous she was moving to le Grande Apple and how sometimes her parents' materialism really made her cringe. I totally got the impression that Sophie's mom was driving the whole party process now, and even in small moments where I could tell Soph was freaking and would rather not push this party competition with Whit, her mom was behind the wheel, full speed ahead. In fact, Sophie and Whitney's moms had been bombarding Ms. Hoffer with calls to secure the January 28 date, and even though Sophie got there first, the Hoffer couldn't fully commit because Mr. Blake was on the board. Finally both mothers ignored her and the stupid book and went ahead as planned, without her approval.

I also had some "seems like old times" times with Whit. We

spent a weekend at her house in Southampton just vegging and watching Will Ferrell movies, chowing down on total junk at every opportunity. I could tell she was also a little stressed about the party, and every time her mom appeared (mostly to monitor our food intake) and had some new development for the bash, Whitney visibly changed. I was sad that Soph and Whit were under so much pressure, but in those moments where we just hung out I had a great time.

The whole thing really got me thinking about parental pressure. It was weird, but even though they were planning this major fete I was kind of glad that I had nothing to do with it. Every day, either Ava or Kaitlin was like a messenger girl, bringing the information about what the other camp was doing. For example, the second that Mrs. Blake booked the Pierre, Mrs. Mitchum booked the Plaza. The day Mrs. Mitchum booked celebrity chef Wolfgang Puck, Mrs. Blake brought in some famous French chef who had like a zillion Michelin stars. When Mrs. Blake arranged for David Copperfield to be jetted in from Monaco, Mrs. Mitchum had a plane for transport and a grand stage custom-made to accommodate Roy's (as in Siegfried and . . .) wheelchair so that he could make his first theatrical appearance since the accident. Kind of gruesome. Nothing was out of reach for them.

The other cool news was that besides my QT with Soph and Whit, I was also having some serious QT with Jake. I felt like we were becoming good pals. We were on the phone, like, every night and it felt fully natch, like he was a girl, but not. It was really odd, because I actually talked to him more than I did Sophie and Whit, who were always out now at night sampling restaurant dishes and theater acts to bring to their party. But I didn't feel like I was missing any sort of companionship because I could totally be myself with Jake, and he and I had an easy time just chatting. Sometimes I would look at the clock and couldn't believe that we'd been on the phone for an hour. And the thing is, we didn't chat about stupid stuff like gossip but about things such as the places we'd most like to visit (I said India and he said the Galápagos Islands) and our favorite movies (I loved *When Harry Met Sally* and he admitted he also thought it rocked. How cool is that, considering most guys like crap with robots?).

We also talked about where we wanted to go to college, and about museum exhibits—it turns out we both loved photography. It was just nice to have a new friend. The only topic that was kind of awkward was Sophie and Whit. They still pressed me at every minute to mention them to him, put in a good word, to try to get them to see him, and every time I brought it up Jake kind of changed the topic. Maybe he was really torn between which one he wanted. I mean, obviously they were both drop-dead gorge, but in such different ways it was probably a nightmare for him to choose. I braced myself every day for the news.

Chapter Eighteen

I never knew a red bouncy dodgeball could be a lethal weapon. The next day in gym class, the battle had begun, and I mean, move over, Braveheart. You should have seen how Whitney and Sophie hurled the cranberry orb in high hopes of pelting the demons out of each other. Ms. Rand's whistle blew, followed by her temper.

"Hey! Cut it out!" she yelled at Sophie, who had just smashed the ball in Whitney's direction. Unfortunately, through Whit's quick moves, the ball ended up bashing poor Molly McGee in the

face. "That's a foul, Mitchum. Let's keep it B the B, below the breasts."

Whitney shot Sophie a look of death and Sophie just taunted her with a huge smile. The piercing whistle blew again and Ms. Rand tossed Whitney the ball. With all her might, she lunged forward and shot it at Sophie with a vengeance that wiped the smile clean off Sophie's face.

"Ow! Ms. Rand!" Sophie screamed, pressing a hand to her cheek. I glanced in Whit's direction long enough to see a satisfied grin.

"You're out of here, Blake. Hit the showers," she ordered. "You, too, Mitchum. This is not a battlefield."

I watched them leave in silence, wondering what the two of them would do in the locker room. The bell interrupted my mental image of their joust, and the rest of us followed suit to the lockers. Ugh. I just wanted to make it to last period and then we would have a week off for Thanksgiving.

"Happy turkey, all of yous. See you next week," Ms. Rand said in her husky voice as we all filed out nervously, wondering what carnage awaited us by the lockers. Surprisingly, it was quiet. By this point, our class was literally divided. Half was on Whit's side of the shower room, the other on Sophie's. The two queen bees had their allegiances in order, and I was the only one who was trying to enter both hives. But the tension and venom were mounting. I was just praying I wasn't going to get stung by being in the middle.

* * *

The next day was Thanksgiving, but before my family chowtime, I was busy with Sophie and then Whitney, as both were concurrently jamming on party plans the whole day and needed my two cents. And, natch, both asked if Jake had mentioned them and whose Sweet Sixteen party he was leaning toward. Afterward, I could not have been more psyched to just get the hell home and plop down to eat. I smiled when I saw my mom had hung on our front door the funny papier-mâché turkey I'd made in second grade. I swear, I mark the year's touchstones not by my Filofax calendar but by whatever "art" my kid self crafted that my mom uses for decoration.

"Honey, is that you?" I heard my mom yell.

"Hiii! Yes, c'est moi. I'm sorry I'm so late." I put my knapsack full of stupid party planning books (homework, said Whitney) down in the small foyer and started to de-layer my pounds of clothing. I heard chatter in the other room and smelled delicious food cooking. "I had to go to Sophie's dress fitting and then to look at photographers' books with Whitney. I can't believe so many people work on Thanksgiving. God, I feel like I'm living a double life!" I walked into the kitchen. And was shocked into silence. Jake Watkins was sitting at my table.

"Here she is," said my dad, kissing me hello as I just stared at Jake, who was up to his elbows in turkey stuffing. He looked gorgeous in his blue button-down and my mom's apron. Uh-oh, *out, out, damn thought!* I am, like, his sis at this point.

"Hi," I said in sort of a zonelike state.

"Finnegan." He smiled.

"Jake is a Cordon Bleu–level chef, my dear," gushed my mom.

"Really?" I asked, still confused as to why Soph and Whit's human tug-of-war was sitting in my kitchen.

"If you're wondering why I'm here," Jake started (oh, he's a mind reader, too), "I called you to wish you a happy Thanksgiving and your mom interviewed me on my holiday plans—"

"And I was devastated to hear Jake was alone for the holiday. So I demanded that he get right down here."

"You're so sweet, Mrs. Finnegan," he said. "You don't know how tired I am of picking up a turkey sandwich at Gardenia and watching too much television."

"And he says he loves mashed turnips, which is music to our ears," said my dad, the king of root vegetables.

"Finally you've found a courageous taster for your concoction, Dad" was all I could mumble.

"Oh, and by the way, that young man called you again," my dad said, looking at a nearby Post-it. "Josh."

I turned red. Josh? Ew! Why was he calling? He had called the night before and had some dumb excuse like he needed Ava's number for someone else, but I knew he just wanted to talk. I had quickly gotten off the phone. But now he had called again, and Jake probably thinks we *chat*! Gross. I looked over at Jake to see his reaction, but unfortunately his back was to me and he was busy chopping veggies. All I could muster was a weak "thanks" to my dad. "I have to go dump the rest of my stuff in my room; be right back," I said.

As I was throwing a brush through my wind-tangled mane, Jake came in.

"Um, listen, if you're bummed out I came, I can totally bolt," said Jake, a little sheepishly. "Or if you have to call Josh back or whatever—"

"What? No, I'm psyched you're here. I was just surprised," I said. *Don't leave*, I wanted to chant.

"Sure? Because I don't want to be a crasher."

"Positive," I said, a little too emphatically. "I mean, I really like having guests. It gets boring just being with the units all the time."

"Better than without them," said Jake. Before I could ask him what the deal was with his MIA 'rents, he changed the subject. "Wow, so this is your fashion design center," he said, examining my piles of fabric, ribbons, and sewing gear.

"Yeah, this is where it all happens, my very unglamorous sweatshop."

"Where are all the Malaysian eleven-year-olds?" he asked. I had to laugh. But my smile was eclipsed by a full-force blush attack as Jake's eyes turned to peruse my walls, which were laden with huge, romantic black-and-white posters of couples kissing, running hand in hand on the Brooklyn Bridge, and the famous post–WWII soldier-nurse smooch in Times Square. Jake stopped in front of the large frame over my bed, my all-time fave photograph of a man and a woman dancing slowly on a New York City rooftop surrounded by twinkling Christmas lights and the majestic skyline in the background. It was the dream image that floated above my brain all night as I slept, and it accompanied all my reveries of one day falling in love.

"I love this photograph," Jake said simply, studying the sliver of silvery moon above the Chrysler Building.

"Isn't it amazing?" I asked. "Especially now, with all the party craziness with my friends. This picture shows me that you don't need the glitz or the booming band or the crowds, that a quiet moment can be enough."

"You're right," Jake said, still gazing at the poster.

"Not to mention that their life looks so damn perfect."

"Your life is pretty perfect," Jake said.

"*My* life?" I asked incredulously. "What are you talking about?"

"I'm talking about you've got it all—"

"Laura! Jake! Dinner!" my dad announced, interrupting him. On the way into the kitchen I wondered about Jake's observation skills. My life perfect? Was he on crack? How could my hovel of an apartment compare to the rest of my classmates' palaces and his swank place as well?

Over burned-down candles, piles of plates, Martinelli's sparkling cider, and pumpkin pie, the four of us talked about Jake's parents being abroad for his dad's board meeting. My dad was asking him all about school, and Jake really opened up about the stress thrown at him by his fam.

"I just feel like I have to accomplish everything my father has and beyond," he confessed.

"That's what I call the burden of privilege," said my dad. "You have a whole different set of pressures; people look at you and project perfection and expect you to follow in a dynasty's footsteps."

"'To whom much has been given, much shall be expected,'" my mom quoted.

"Everyone wants me to be on all the varsity teams and go to Princeton like my whole family, be number one," Jake said. "I told my parents I wanted to be an architect and they freaked. They said it wasn't a socially acceptable profession for families like ours. What does that even mean?"

"But what about the people who have the same pressure as you along with the additional pressure to keep up financially?" I asked, kind of indignant. All these wealthy kids and their "problems." I knew they were real, but sometimes I was like, *Cry me a river.* "I'm sorry, Jake, I know that set of issues is all very real to you, but I'm on a free ride at Tate and that has even more 'burdens.'"

"Trust me, I'm not crying poor Jake," he protested. "I'm just saying that the world can be oppressive and claustrophobic sometimes."

"Well, luckily everyone at this table has been blessed with so much good fortune. Think of all the people in this world—on the streets of our own city—who don't get to sit down to a nice meal with good company. We are infinitely lucky." My mom took my hand and Jake's in hers and squeezed. Then she blew a kiss to my dad, who mime-caught it. Ugh. Jake must think my family is so Woodstock.

After dessert, I walked Jake down to our stoop, semi-nervous because I had promised Sophie that morning that I'd make a plan for Saturday that included Jake.

"I had a great time," said Jake, sounding grateful.

"Listen, Jake, there's something I need to ask you—"

"Shoot."

"Um, Sophie wanted to know if you're free Saturday night for a mini-soiree at her place."

Jake looked down at his shoes. "Are you going?"

"Yeah."

He paused. "Okay."

"Great! I mean, she'll be so psyched. It's going to be really fun."

Jake looked like he was about to say something else but then stopped and said, "Tonight was a lot of fun."

"I'm so glad you came. It was such a fun surprise."

Jake looked at me and I looked back at him. For a moment I almost thought he was going to kiss me. I guess I was swept away by all that cider. But after a pause it looked like he remembered something, probably his darling love interests, Sophie and Whit.

So he zipped up his jacket and turned on his way.

"Good night, Finnegan," he said over his shoulder.

"Good night, Jake."

I turned to watch him disappear down the tree-lined block and felt a pang of crushdom, which I quickly gulped down. *Yeah, right, Laura,* I thought. *Take a number.*

Chapter Nineteen

I was right not to get my hopes up. Okay, I actually did get my hopes up, and they were totally destroyed, which is why I have to keep reminding my idiotic self never to get my hopes up. Sometimes I just get sooo carried away in my romantic daydreams, and I thought I maybe had a slight chance with Jake post–turkey bonding, but then Sophie's mini-soiree confirmed that he was way out of my league. The whole night was a barf-inducing nightmare, and I really wished I had a) never gone, and b) never invited Jake. Blech.

Sophie had invited Kaitlin and me over to get ready early. Her friend Allie Brosnan was visiting from L.A., so she was also there when I arrived. I had worn a vintage '40s print dress that I had picked up in a thrift store and had tailored perfectly, if I do say so myself, with some cool Jane Mayle wedge shoes that I had splurged on. I borrowed some of my mom's retro Bakelite jewelry (Who'd have thought that she'd collect something that actually came back in style?) and was feeling pretty good about my outfit. But when I watched Allie, Sophie, and Kaitlin get ready in full designer duds, I started to feel out of place immediately. I could tell that Allie followed the Sophie manner of dressing and lifestyle more than my own, and Kaitlin was quickly following suit. I don't want to say slutty, but they were all on the more promiscuous side of things. I watched as they slid their bodies into skintight spaghetti-strap tanks (it was 30 degrees outside, meanwhile) and übershort cutoff jean skirts. If they bent over, you could literally see their thongs. They put on ultra-high shoes by D&G, Versace, and Prada, so thin-heeled that they could barely walk. And on top of that, they all wore a ton of makeup.

The guys arrived at 8:00. Josh immediately started firing away at me with stupid stories, so before I could even say hi to Jake, he was swept off by Sophie to meet Allie. I watched them out of the corner of my eye and felt weirdly jealous. Sophie was totally territorial about Jake, as if she were introducing Allie to her boyfriend. Why did I always have to be the one to mediate, to be the good guy, to calm everyone down and sacrifice everything I wanted? I mean, here I was, stuck talking to the biggest loser, and the man of my dreams is being paraded around by one of my so-called best friends? Just once it would be nice to not always have to be the good girl and take the moral high road. What I really wanted to do was grab Jake's hand and dash out of there. But alas, I couldn't bring myself to do that.

Later that night, after plates and plates of tapas served by Sophie's chef (read: plates with barely any food on them), we retired to the library, where the boys started playing video games (Sophie always had the newest releases before they were even on the shelves, but she didn't even play them) and the girls chatted. Finally, after several wine coolers, Sophie gathered everyone in a circle and placed an empty bottle in the center. She winked at Allie (who she was clearly matchmaking with Bobby) and cleared her voice to get everyone's attention.

"Okay, listen. So it's like spin the bottle, where the bottle decides your fate. But instead of macking in front of everyone like Kaitlin and Max, you go to the closet for three minutes," said Sophie triumphantly, as if she had just explained quantum physics.

"I've heard of that game," said Bobby. "It's called Three Minutes in Heaven."

"Well, we don't call it that on the coast," said Sophie impatiently. "Okay, who should go first? Laura?"

"Um, no thanks," I said, turning bright red.

"We all have to go," said Josh eagerly.

"I realize that, but I'd rather not go first," I said curtly. I was fed up with him.

"This is dumb," said Jake. Thank you!

"Shut up, let's play," said Josh. His enthusiasm made me feel dirty.

"Why don't you start, Sophie? It's your house," said Max.

"Fine," said Sophie confidently. She was definitely game. She spun the bottle and, as if by magic, it pointed directly at Jake. Sophie beamed. "Well."

"Dude!" snorted Bobby.

"See ya guys!" yelled Max. "B-bye!"

"Score," added Josh. He was always a beat late.

I looked at Jake, who didn't betray any emotion. God, he was so good at maintaining a poker face. There was just no way to read that guy.

"Shall we?" asked Sophie, rising.

Jake sat for a second. At first I thought he wasn't going to move. My heart leaped. Maybe he doesn't want to kiss her! Maybe he will stand up and profess his love for me! Just when I started to get carried away, he finally stood up and followed Sophie out of the room. I wanted to throw up.

"Well, I bet we'll be here longer than three minutes. Let's turn on the tube," said Bobby, flicking on the remote.

"Or we could keep playing?" said Allie suggestively, taking the remote out of Bobby's hands. What is it about California girls? New meaning to the word "joystick."

"We should wait," I said.

Josh turned to me. "So, have you ever played this before, Finnegan?" He made me cringe when he called me that. I mean, when Jake called me that I literally got tingles, but when Josh said it, it just seemed so poser-ish. He was completely incapable of thinking for himself. A total NOTL.

"No," I said.

"Well, don't worry. I'll be prepared," Josh said, whipping out Binaca and spraying his mouth. *Ew!*

"Um, I have to go to the bathroom," I said, popping up.

I walked through the foyer by the closet on my way to the bathroom. There was no light shining out from under the door. Obviously Sophie and Jake were fully going at it. Yuck. I wanted to barf. After splashing water on my face and lingering in the bathroom to avoid Josh, I walked back and again saw no light on in the closet.

"How'd it go?" asked Josh.

"How'd what go?"

"The bathroom?"

"Um, fine, thanks." Loser.

I sat down next to Kaitlin, who leaned in and whispered, "They aren't back yet! I'm so happy for Sophie; she's been wanting this for sooooo long."

"Yeah, it's great," I said, feigning joy.

"What do you think about Allie and Bobby? She's nice but seems like a slut. I mean, she barely knows him," said Kaitlin, making a face. Talk about the pot calling the kettle black.

"Whatever," I said.

Just then Sophie and Jake came back in the room. Sophie was buttoning her blouse and looked flushed, but when she looked around the room and saw that everyone was staring, she broke into a huge grin. Immediately the guys started howling and making catcalls.

"Shall we continue?" asked Sophie.

"Who's next?" said Allie, obviously eager to have a turn.

"Laura's next, but Jake has to sit this one out since he just had a turn," said Sophie quickly.

Of course. Sophie couldn't risk anyone else getting a chance to kiss Jake. This scenario was getting worse and worse.

"Is that really the way it works, Sophie?" asked Jake.

I looked over at him with surprise. Did that mean that Jake wanted a chance to kiss me? Or was he just a stickler for the rules?

"Yes, I'm afraid that's the house rule," said Sophie.

Great. So this was my life now. It was the definition of peer pressure. I didn't want to participate in this charade, but I felt disempowered to bail. I shrugged and spun the bottle halfheartedly. It landed directly between Josh and Max.

"Looks like Josh to me," said Bobby.

"Me too," said Max.

Was this a conspiracy? Someone call Oliver Stone.

"Let's go, Laura," said Josh, offering his hand to pull me up. I didn't take it. I just couldn't deal with clasping a sweaty hand to pretend that he's a knight in shining armor. I followed him to the closet, preparing a speech in my head. The second we got in, he turned off the light and I turned it back on again.

"Josh . . . ," I began. But before I could finish, he lunged in for a kiss. I was startled but finally pushed him away. His breath smelled disgusting, like garlic Binaca.

"Stop," I said, pushing him away harder.

"I've been waiting for this," said Josh. He tried to kiss me again, but I put my hand up and jerked my head away. "And I know you have too, Finnegan."

"I'm sorry, Josh. I just . . . I like you, but not in that way."

"What do you mean?" he asked testily.

"I just want to be friends," I said. Whew. That was easier than I thought.

"But you flirt with me all the time," he said, his voice turning angry.

"Excuse me?"

"You totally lead me on!" I had never seen Josh so pissed.

"I'm sorry if you think that; that was never my intention. I totally don't think I lead you on."

"You're a little tease. Nice, Finnegan," he said, shoving open the door and storming out. I'd never heard my name said with such venom. I followed Josh back into the library. I think everyone could tell my face was pale and Josh looked angry. But as soon as he realized everyone was waiting for his reaction, he tried to put on a show, as if he was Mr. Cool Man, and high-fived

Bobby. I was furious, and Sophie could tell something was up.

"Um, Laura, could you help me in the kitchen?" she said, grabbing my arm and pulling me out of the room.

We walked down the hall into the kitchen. "So, what happened?" Sophie asked breathlessly. "Did you and Josh finally smooch?"

"Disgusting, Sophie, no. You all know I don't like him. He is such a dork. Why does everyone try to push us to be a couple?"

"You're right. You are so above him. You shouldn't waste your time. We'll find you someone way better."

"Yeah . . . ," I said, thinking that my Way Better just made out with her. "So how'd it go with Jake?" I asked, trying to be casual. Trying not to chunder.

"I have to say, amazing," she said, smiling from ear to ear as my heart sank slowly. "He is so sweet, and such an awesome kisser. I'm still rushing from it!"

"That's great," I managed to muster.

Sophie looked at me and could see I was bummed, but she thought it was because of Josh, not Jake. "Don't worry, Laura, your birthday is in a month and I'm determined to find you a real man by then. I'm going to scan my BlackBerry tonight and see who we can set you up with. Hey, I think Elijah Wood is single!"

"Yeah, as if," I said, dejected. I grabbed an apple and took a bite.

"You never know," said Sophie. "It will be my mission to hook you up."

"Thanks," I said. At this point, the only man I wanted was in her arms.

While Sophie was euphoric, floating through the next few days on cloud nine, I did my best to keep the news from Whitney. I felt a little dishonest, seeing as she was my BF, but if she didn't ask me directly what I did on Saturday or if Sophie and Jake had happened to make out over the weekend, then there was no point in offering that information unsolicited. And seeing as Whitney was still in extreme party planning mode, it didn't look like it would come up.

I was trying to study for my history final in the library when Whitney came bursting in, pushing aside my flashcards to show me the latest sketch of her dress.

"It's beautiful, Whit," I said.

"So, um, have you happened to see Sophie's?" asked Whitney, trying to be casual.

"Yeah," I said. Here we go. "And it's nice too."

"Whatever," said Whitney, flipping her hair. "Her party will suck."

"Whitney, can you finally just get over this and make up? This fight is so juvenile, and it's taking over everything."

"No thanks, it's not happening."

I sighed. After a while this just got so boring. "Okay, then do what you have to do."

"I will. My party is full speed ahead, and no way will trailer trash ever darken the doorway of my ball. I don't even want to think about her."

"Okay, you're talking like a crazy person. I'm just going to continue to stay out of it." Which was getting harder and harder.

"Do what you want. I just know you'll be at my party."

I didn't want to tell her I was planning on going to both. But both parties seemed so remote right now. I was more concerned with nursing a semi-broken heart that I wished I had been strong enough to control so I wouldn't be in this position. I mean, damn, it's just a little muscle; why did it ache so much?

The little boat I had been diplomatically sailing between the two islands of Sophie and Whitney so far had definitely seen some shaky waters. But the sharks were circling and my boat was about to capsize. I would later learn why both Whitney and Sophie turned on me.

It turns out Whit and her mom had gone for dinner to La Grenouille to discuss party details. They had been having a totally normal time when Whitney looked up to see a horrified look on her mom's face.

"That is an *affront*!" Mrs. Blake ranted. "They should not be allowed in here."

Whitney turned to see an extremely obese family sitting down to dinner at the adjacent banquette.

"Mother—"

"Don't *Mother* me. How can people let themselves go like that? Get some self-control!"

"Maybe it's not their fault," Whitney attempted. "Maybe it's their genes or something?"

"Well, if my DNA fails me like that, you just take one of daddy's Holland & Holland silver shotguns and kill me right there," Mrs. Blake said, gulping a swig of Chardonnay.

"Mom, they can hear you!" Whitney protested.

"Ugh, I think I can see a hint of orange Cheeto dust on the man's face! Appalling. Simply odious." Mrs. Blake waved over the maître d', who was walking by. "Philippe? *Cheri, qui sont les gens ici?*"

"La Famille Couchard. Zey invented zee Bacon Bits."

Mrs. Blake dismissed Philippe and turned to her daughter with solemn eyes. "Whitney," she started calmly. "I want you to look good and hard at those bacon people. I want you to examine them. Because if you keep eating the way you have been, *that*, my dear, will be you."

Whitney felt shame and heat rise to her cheeks. She dropped her hot roll onto her plate and set down the butter knife as if it were a poison-dipped spear.

"Now, when are you picking up the Save the Date cards from the calligrapher?" Mrs. Blake asked, changing the subject. "Have Laura fetch them; she's downtown—"

"Well, she's in the West Village, Mom. It's not that close to Wall Street . . ."

"Downtown is downtown. She can get them."

"I think she's helping Sophie with something tomorrow anyway."

There was a long pause. *"What?"* Mrs. Blake said, venom dripping off her tongue.

"It's okay, Mom. She's trying to stay out of it all," Whitney defended.

"No. It is not 'okay.' After everything we have done for her! All the trips, hand-me-downs, dresses, trinkets, and baubles, and she is aligning herself with that vulturous slag?"

"Mom, Laura doesn't want to be in the middle. It's not that she's on Sophie's side, she's just neutral!"

"She is not Switzerland. A girl in her situation should be more prudent. One cannot have wishy-washy double agents like that in one's life."

"But, Mom . . ."

"Get rid of her."

Similarly, Mrs. Mitchum and Sophie were dining together as their chef served a Chinese dinner—Cantonese, not Szechuan—when Sophie was forced to make a disturbing choice. I later was told the blow-by-blow.

"They lost everything—the Rolls, the twelve-carat diamond, their beloved El Greco—everything!" Adriana apparently gushed.

"But isn't she your friend?" Sophie asked.

"Well, not anymore. Plus, we were never close, really."

"You were in each other's wedding."

Adriana put her chopsticks down. "Sophie," she said as though she were speaking to a small child, "there is a time and a place for friendship. If there's one thing you have to learn in life, it's that you always have to upgrade. Now, that may sound harsh to you, but it is how the world works. And friends embroiled in scandal are like a wart: They must be removed."

"Anyway," said Sophie, switching gears. "I need the driver tomorrow 'cause Laura and I are going to pick out the confetti from that confetti designer in Queens."

"I like that Laura," Mrs. Mitchum mused breezily, crunching into a steamed snowpea. "Good for her to have the smarts to stick with you."

"Well, actually . . . ," Sophie started, "she's still friends with Whitney. She kind of wanted to stay out of the whole fight thing."

Sophie's mom froze. "*What?* She should be on your side! Life is about loyalty!"

"But—"

"I get it, she's a *user*!"

"She's not, she's—"

"Dispensable. That's what she is. It's time to erase her."

Sophie sat quietly, thinking.

"I'm serious," said Adriana stoically. "It's time to flush her down the toilet. Like diarrhea."

Who says parents are mature and always take the high road?

It all went down at the Temple of Dendur, that looming structure that takes up a huge glassed-in chunk of the Metropolitan Museum of Art. We were on a class trip, and I was blissfully unaware that my fate would change that day as I stood, sketch pad in hand, intently listening to the docent explain how this thousands-of-years-old temple ended up in the middle of New York City. When the group dispersed to scribble down some notes, Whitney pulled me off to the side.

"Laura, I have to talk to you," she said. Uh-oh, I knew that face. It was all squished up and her mouth was twitching. Whit always got like that when someone said something offensive to her. I was in trouble.

"Okay . . ." Heart palpitations quickening.

"Is it true you were at Sophie's house and Sophie and Jake made out?" she asked with fury in her voice.

"Yes . . . ," I said.

"Why did you neglect to tell me this?" she asked in a rage.

"Look, Whitney, I knew you'd get all upset, and I just didn't want to be the messenger."

"How could you not tell me? Aren't you my best friend?"

"Yes, but come on, Whitney, do you even like Jake?" I was defensive but also angry. If only Jake knew he was being used as a pawn, he would just freak out and wash his hands of both Sophie and Whitney.

Before Whitney could respond, Sophie came storming up and grabbed my arm. "Laura, we have to talk," she announced, not even acknowledging Whitney.

"Tell the little social-climbing upstart to back off, we're in the middle of a convo," said Whitney.

"This can't wait," snapped Sophie.

"Guys—," I began before Whitney interrupted me.

"I can't really deal with *this*," she said, motioning to Sophie and drawing out the word *this* as if it were polluted.

"I've decided that it is time for you to make a choice," said Sophie, her voice tight but stern.

"There is no choice, Hollywood Trash. Laura is my friend and always will be," Whitney said, addressing Sophie. Then she turned to me. "Laura, I want you to renounce your friendship with Sophie right now. We go much further back, my family and I have done a lot for you, and you can no longer stay friends with her."

I was speechless. *What?* Done *a lot* for me? Was I living in a communist country? What is up with the dictatorship in the friend category? Psycho. But before I could respond, Sophie jumped in.

"She's right about one thing, and only one thing, Laura; it's time to take a side, and I know you'll take mine. I mean, look at what Whitney just said to you. She acts like she *owns* you. She obviously didn't get the news flash that slavery ended fifty years ago," said Sophie.

Um, more like 150 years ago, but okay.

"You guys, this is crazy," I insisted. "I told you from the beginning, I am not taking sides. I'm friends with both of you."

I saw Sophie momentarily waver, but then it looked like she remembered something and she got all serious again. "No, Laura, choose or lose, and I don't mean the Senate race."

"I won't. I'm friends with both of you and that's that."

"No, Laura, you can't be friends with both of us. That is unacceptable," said Whitney, sounding more like her mother every second. "You're not Switzerland. And quite frankly, I don't have time for wafflers!"

"Whit . . ."

Whitney's face started to contort. "The fact that it's not an automatic decision for you proves that you were never really a true friend. You're an opportunist, just like my mother said. You always borrow things, and you're such a user."

I felt like I was being stung by a trillion hornets. "Whoa, Whitney, you're the one who always said what's mine is yours," I said, my voice breaking as I choked back hot tears.

"I didn't mean it literally."

"Decide now, Laura," snapped Sophie. "It's time for you to prove that you're really *my* friend and don't just want to go to premieres."

"If you pick Sophie, I'll know it's just because you want to meet Matt Damon. User." Whitney sneered.

"You'll never meet him at this point," seethed Sophie. "And I'm going to text-message him and tell him what an ugly lesbo you are."

Suddenly I burst into tears. I couldn't believe what I was hearing, that my two "best friends" were turning on me and accusing me of such horrible things. Here I thought I was so mature and had taken the high road, trying to mend their relationship, refusing to backstab them, just staying out of harm's way, and it was all coming back to slap me in the face. Twice.

"You guys, this is so unfair," I sputtered between sobs. "I just didn't want to pick sides!"

"You are so spineless! I'm flushing you down the toilet,"

Sophie said bitterly. "Like diarrhea."

"Laura, your birthday is in three weeks. At the rate you're going, it's going to be Table for One at your crap restaurant 'party,'" hissed Whitney.

Whitney turned to stomp away but then whipped around and spat out one more insult. "And by the way, I'll see to it that Oscar de la Renta *never* sees your stupid dress sketches!" she said, and stomped off.

I looked at Sophie imploringly.

"And ditto for Calvin. And not only that, Miss Vanilla Ice Cream, I'll make sure that Jake and all the other guys *never* talk to you again!" Sophie blurted in a venom-steeped voice before storming away.

I was stunned. I was heartbroken. I was nauseous. And I was angry.

After somehow making it through the rest of the day thinking I was going to have a coronary at any second, I stumbled my way down to the philosophy building at NYU in a haze of grief to find my father. I waited outside his classroom, watching him motion to the students and scribble on the chalkboard while he lectured. After waiting for everyone to file out, I opened the door and went in.

My cute dad was sitting at his desk in his tweed blazer with the usual lunch crumbs all over it, rubbing his glasses with his handkerchief. I couldn't even say hi without bursting into choking sobs. I wept uncontrollably, the hot tears flooding down my cheeks. My dad just took me in his arms and hugged me until I was able to speak. Then, just as I opened my mouth, he put his finger up to tell me to wait, went to the hall, and came back with a paper cup filled with water. I drank it down and finally breathed.

"What happened, sweetie?"

The word *sweetie* set me off again, so after another breakdown, I finally calmed down again and was able to fill him in. "I never knew being called Switzerland was so bad," I finished.

"I'm sure they didn't mean it," said my dad.

"Yes, they did!" I cried, still heaving with sobs. "They promised to ruin my life. All I wanted was to stay out of it, and now I'm *totally* out of it."

I rambled on and on, the stress of the past few weeks spilling out of me. I told him how hard it was for me to be around such rich girls who got everything they ever wanted, how I hated that Whitney threw her generosity back in my face, and how my friends had just made me feel like total crap for trying to stay out of this. I was a total wreck. I felt like all my good intentions had been mocked and that these girls, whom I had only tried to reconcile and remain friends with, had been more evil to me than if they had been my worst enemies. I ended with the statement "And I don't want a birthday party."

That's where my father finally interjected.

"Wait, honey. Your birthday is still a few weeks away. I'm sure things will have settled by then. You can't ignore your Sweet Sixteen. It's a cultural landmark."

"No one will come. I'm a social leper."

"Your mom and I still want to hang out with you."

My dad smiled at me and the tears started again.

"Thanks, Dad. But just be prepared to be the only people singing 'Happy Birthday.'"

"Then we'll just sing it extra loud," said my dad, kissing me on the forehead. "But I promise you, sweetheart, by Monday, at the latest, this will all be over."

Chapter Twenty-two

It had been a quiet weekend. I mean, mute. Crickets. For some reason I expected Whitney and Sophie to call and apologize, telling me they were crazy and it was all a bad dream and let's just forget about it. But nothing. Silence. The only person who called was Jake, but luckily I wasn't there. I mean, I would love to download it all to Jake, but I was a) secretly worried that Whitney or Sophie had already filled him in, spinning it to their advantage, in which case he'd be repulsed; or b) afraid that he knew nothing and I would have to fill him in on the humiliating fact that I was now friendless. A loser.

I hate that panicky feeling you get when you are in a big fight with your best friends. It's like being solo on a desert island. I don't need people bashing me behind my back. And the more I thought about it, the more it really pissed me off that they were unable to see my side of things.

Move over, Reese Witherspoon in *Election*. On Monday Whitney and Sophie were burning up the campaign trail to get everyone in our grade to come to their rival Sweet Sixteen bashes. I never knew free loot could buy friendship. When I walked in that morning, I saw I was an even bigger pariah than I'd suspected. Every single person—and I mean nerds whom I was always nice to but Whitney snubbed—was being courted. Every Whit-proclaimed "geek," "loser," and "total NOTL" was now being begged to attend her party, only because it was one less geek Sophie could claim as her guest. They were like chess pawns, only they had acne and clear braces.

"Ding!" Round one commenced. In one corner, Sophie was handing out T-shirts that said SOPHIE'S 16! SAVE THE DATE! On the other side of the lounge, Whitney started handing out little blue Tiffany boxes. Everyone ripped their gifts open to find sterling key chains with Whitney's date of birth on the back and her monogram on the other, all hand-engraved. It was a turf war zone, like *West Side Story* minus the dancing.

"Hey, Belle!" Whitney smiled, newly BriteSmile-bleached tusks gleaming. "Here ya go, Susie!"

Nice. She had called both Belle and Susie "bison" the week before. After handing another ribbon-tied box to Lily Baxter (whom she used to call 'Limi Baxter because of her bout with bu*limi*a), Whitney caught me looking her way. She shot me a glare from Hades and walked off. Ouch—her poisonous gaze was like a laser and killed what was left of my nerves to hell. My sweet parents swore this would "all wear off," but I didn't see any love coming my way anytime soon. As much as I wanted to confront her and Sophie, my anger was dwarfed by my fear of the evil dopplegängers they had become.

Plus the pranks between Sophie and Whitney had definitely ratcheted up since the whole boot-out-Laura thing. First, after a class where we had been learning about mythological beasts, Whitney scanned a picture of Sophie onto her computer and grafted Sophie's head onto a horse's body, making her a Sophie centaur. Then she printed out copies and gave them to everyone. To top it off, Whit's group started whinnying when Sophie walked by. You could tell Sophie was enraged. Then, later, I saw "WHITNEY = PIG" scrawled in Yves St. Laurent lipstick on Whit's locker. She tried to laugh it off, then opened it to find a cache of fetal pigs Sophie had purloined from Mr. Rosenberg's laboratory. As horrifying and gut-churning as the swine guts galore were, the stench was worse. (The noxious cocktail of ballet-slipper stink coupled with formaldehyde lingered in the hall, impossible to expunge. All the Miu Miu coats had to go.)

Whitney's screams were met with sympathy as the war heated

up even more. I knew she was more furious than she'd ever been. And I also knew that major retribution was not far behind. I shuddered to think what it would be, almost grateful at this point for my ex-friend status.

I got through Monday the way a soldier gets through a trench: by lying low and dodging the bullets as best he can. The thing was, even though Ava and Kaitlin and all of my other friends were normal to me, Whitney and Sophie were such powerhouses that it seemed like the entire class was against me. People still *talked* to me, but there wasn't exactly a line to be my new best friend. The fact was that the competing birthday parties were so dominating our class that a) no one wanted to risk alienating one of the birthday girls for fear they wouldn't be invited, so they limited their interaction with me, and b) all anyone talked about these days was the birthday parties, and now that they knew I was on the blacklist, why bother talking to me? I felt much more like Tom Hanks in *Cast Away* every second.

I didn't truly exhale until I burst out of the double doors and spilled my carcass onto the street. Soft snowflakes were starting to float down from the sky and the scent of Christmas trees was in the air. This was normally my favorite time of year. I really got into all the holiday decorations and everything, totally NOTL-y, but this year I couldn't even enjoy that, with all the stress in my life. It was only a week until Christmas break and the Gold and Silver Ball, which I had been so psyched for and was now dreading.

Every year, the first weekend of Christmas break is the all-important Gold and Silver Ball. It is of mega-significance because it's not just our class but tenth through twelfth grades from all the private schools. It's held at the Waldorf-Astoria hotel on Park Avenue, and the street out front is glutted with limos and Cadillac Escalades, drivers perched at the wheel, ready to shuttle their teen clients to various after-parties up and down Fifth Avenue, hoping they don't chunder in the backseat.

As I walked toward the bus stop with my head down, I spied with my peripheral vision Sophie and her new posse (Ava and a few other girls who Sophie had never talked to before) in the diner, munching fries with their feet up, hanging in the corner table I always used to plop down in after school. I saw her shoot me a slit-eyed glare through the window, and I am sure if the glass wasn't there I would have keeled over. My fast walk turned to a trot as I closed in on the bus stop where hopefully an M4 would pull up and take me away from all the unpleasantness, all the tears, and all the terror of Tate. Seven more days until break, thank God—I wished I could reach into the future and pull myself there right away.

As a big blue bus started to pull up, I heard a familiar voice.

"Finnegan!"

"Hey, Jake." I couldn't even bear to look him in the eye.

"I've been yelling your name for blocks!"

"Sorry, I guess I was in the zone," I said, taking a deep breath.

"You're always in the zone! Geez, it's like you turn on your deaf ears when you walk to your bus."

I could tell he was just trying to be funny, but I wasn't in a laughing mood. He noticed right away.

"How come you haven't returned my phone calls?" he asked, cheeks flushed from running up to me.

"Sorry," I said kind of coldly. "I have exams. Not to mention a little social chaos."

"Listen, Laura, I know you're going out with Josh and all, but—"

"What?" Was he insane? Not if Josh was the last humanoid roaming the green orb we call earth.

Jake looked momentarily annoyed. "He told me about, you know . . ."

"About *what*?"

"That you guys hooked up at Sophie's, and last weekend."

My blood was bubbling its way up to my face. "That is a *total lie*!"

Jake looked surprised. "That's what Josh said . . ."

"He's lying."

"Oh." He said it in a tone that I wasn't familiar with. Was he happy? Was he indifferent? I couldn't tell. We stared at each other for a second.

The bus opened its doors as a line formed to board.

"So . . . why haven't you called me back?" Jake asked earnestly.

I dug through my bag, which was a bottomless pit of pencils, scraps, pennies, and paper clips, searching for my bus pass. "I told you, things have been crazy." Well, it was true. Things *had* been crazy, what with my being a social leper 'n' all. But then I thought, Screw it, my life is in shambles anyway, I might as well go down in flames. "Plus, Jake, I really didn't want to interrupt one of your rolls in the hay with Sophie." I spat that out.

"What are you talking about?" he asked.

"Look, I have enough heinosity in my life right now, I don't even want to explain. I'll talk to you later." I finally retrieved my bus pass and climbed the stairs as Jake stood on the sidewalk.

"So that's it, Finnegan? You're blowing me off? Friendship over?"

Just hearing him say the word "friendship" made me even sicker. "I don't know, Jake," I said, flashing my student pass to the driver as the doors began to close him out. "I don't know about anything anymore."

Chapter Twenty-three

Should I have been so harsh to Jake? No. It was inexcusable. But I was sick of being his "friend" and listening to all his problems with his parents and hearing him tell me how he wants to be an architect and all his other taxicab confessions, only to have him go off and make out with Sophie. I mean, I know we were playing spin the bottle and he had no choice, but he clearly enjoyed it, according to her. And now it just seemed like he was leading me on. I didn't want to play the role of "best friend" anymore. It was getting too painful.

And the more I thought about it, the more pissed off I got. At Jake, for leading me on. And for not liking me. At Whitney, for being my so-called best friend for years and then dumping me at the drop of a hat. At Sophie, for butting into our clique and then making a mess of everything. And at my parents, for sending me to that lion's den where they had to know that one day not being able to keep up with the silverspoon set would really matter, despite how well I did academically. And since they were ten feet away in the kitchen, I ended up channeling all of my venom toward them. They were an easy target and were still currently speaking to me, but also they had dropped me in that situation in the first place.

They could definitely tell I was ticked off when I sat down to dinner, glowering. I saw my father and mother exchange what they thought were discreet raised eyebrows at each other and I decided to let them know how angry I was.

"You know, Mom and Dad, you guys are really to blame for all this," I announced, placing my glass of milk down on the table with a dramatic thud.

"What do you mean, sweetheart?" asked my mom, perplexed.

"It's, like, I was a baby fish and you dropped me into a tank full of sharks."

"Is Tate the fish tank?" asked my father, scratching his head.

"Yup."

My parents gave each other one of those "we are so much wiser than her" looks that make me want to murder. They took a collective deep breath.

"Honey, this seems like misdirected anger," said my mother. "I think you know how wonderful Tate has been for you, and the value of a great education, Miss A's on her last two term papers."

"And don't forget, you and Whitney have been best friends for years," said my dad. "This might be a momentary fissure in your friendship, but I have no doubt you will reunite and be best pals again."

"I don't think so," I said, folding my arms. "I can't even remember *why* I was friends with her in the first place. She's spoiled and self-centered. So not fun."

"Whitney? Come on," coaxed my mom. "I remember all the fun times you girls had when you were little, putting on musicals for me and Daddy, going to all those gymnastics classes together. You were two goofballs!"

That Whitney seemed so different from the Whitney I currently knew. It's true, we had a lot of fun together when we were younger. In first grade we used to sit in the corner of our homeroom and draw horses over and over and compete with other girls over whose was the best, until the head of lower school got fed up and banned drawing horses. And then in third grade our teacher Mrs. Palmer used to let us out of class early so we could race home and watch *General Hospital*. (Yes, soap operas are really for the very young, and we were totally addicted.) In fifth grade we spent hours rehearsing our tap-dance routine to "Macarena." In sixth grade we spent every free moment for three weeks writing, choreographing, and composing a musical version of *The Parent Trap*. I could go on and on . . . but it just seemed like that Whitney didn't exist anymore. Things like money and country clubs and private planes, things that don't matter to you when you are little, all seemed so important to her now and had made the abyss between us grow. I used to fool myself that she could ignore it, but unfortunately she had proven me wrong. Dead wrong.

"Whitney's changed," I said, suddenly realizing what the years had done to my friend. "She's turned into her mother."

"Whitney may be going through something right now and be very caught up in it, but you have to remember why you liked her in the first place. She'll come around again," said my mom.

Why I liked her in the first place was becoming a distant memory. I know when people bashed her I always defended her, saying although she may seem stuck up and snobby, she was just insecure because her mother always did a number on her, telling her she was too fat or that she slouched. Harp, harp, harp, that's all her mother does. Her mother is way too concerned with the superficial—that's one reason why Whitney is such a mess, especially recently, with all the party planning. But how could I defend her anymore when she was being evil to *me*? Before I could say anything, it was as if my father read my mind.

"Laura, I know it is not reassuring to say that this will end, and that you and Whitney will one day be friends again—"

"No, we won't," I interrupted.

"Well, I'm not sure I can believe that. You've had too many good times," said my mom, dishing out more green beans. "And what about Sophie?"

"She's lame too. *I* was the one who defended her to Whitney and everyone else. They all said she was vapid and vain, but I insisted that she was not all flash, that yes she was fun on a superficial level, but she had heart. *I* brought her into our group and she turned it upside down. I can't believe I brought it on myself."

"Oh, honey, you were only trying to make her feel welcome," said my dad, putting his hand on top of mine. "There's nothing wrong with that."

"I guess. But it totally backfired. I wanted her and Whitney to be friends because I thought that they were two peas in a pod. Once you break through their outer facades they're on the same level and can be fun to talk to and go out with. But the problem was exactly that. They were too similar, and they are both small-minded and shallow."

My parents could tell I was about to cry, so they sat in silence, giving me sympathetic looks and caressing my arm. What I hated most of all was that Whitney and Sophie made me feel like I was using them. They think someone like me, someone without as much money, would just covet those fancy clothes and love those trips abroad and all that. But I've grown up around it so much that I am used to not having it. And Whitney was always cool about sharing her clothes, but at the same time I was soooo hyper-careful about not being a mooch and had even made a niche for myself designing my own duds. And for every trip to the Caribbean that she took me on, there were ten that I declined. She had zero frigging right to make me seem like an opportunist.

"You feel betrayed," my mom said as if she were reading my mind.

"I just . . ." I started to cry, and my parents both hugged me. Finally I took a breath. "I guess it *does* bother me that I don't have all this money and stuff. And I thought as long as we were friends it didn't matter, but now that we aren't and I'm, like, ostracized by everyone, it all just seems like a class thing. It's like 'You can come in if we let you in, but we have every right to throw you out.' And I just feel . . . so alone and dumb. Dumb for even caring about this crap when I should be studying for my math exam."

"Laura, you're not alone," said my dad. "I know it can be rough being a loner or an outsider, but trust me, it will turn out okay. Everything will work out."

I choked back tears. "Thanks . . ."

"And you always have Daddy and me to be goofballs with," said my mom, gently pushing my hair out of my eyes.

We had a group hug before I went into my room for the night. I hoped that things would get better. But could all these feelings of anger and hurt and rejection and embarrassment ever be reconciled? I doubted it. It's like when you're sick and in the depths of the fever, you truly feel like you'll never get well. You just have to power through and take one hour at a time.

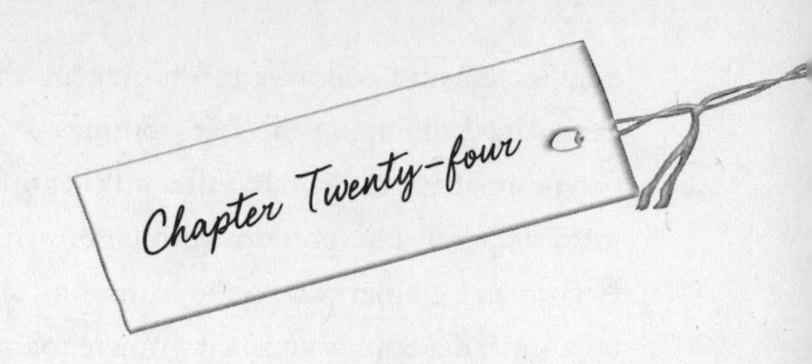

It's almost scary how easy it is to be invisible. The next day at school I threw myself into study mode, crunching for my exams and trying at all costs to avoid everyone. And it was strangely simple. I glided around, laying low and doing my own thing. I would be lying if I said my heart didn't skip a few beats when I heard Sophie and her posse or Whitney and crew strolling by, but they generally ignored me.

At one point, I was in the library and heard two freshmen freaking out. From their conversation I was able to make out that

Sophie had just sabotaged Whitney in the cafeteria—the ol' chocolate-pudding-on-the-seat routine. When Whit and her gang came back to her table after a Pellegrino refill, she slid right into the goo and got up with a brown blob on her butt. Nightmare! On her way to the bathroom, she apparently walked by a smirking Sophie and said, "You're toast."

Ugh. Between the death threats, lame pranks, and my honors algebra 2 test, I was drowning in stress. The feng shui of Tate was all off and I was immersed in bad vibes with only an hour till test time.

"And . . . *stop*." Mr. Caster's voice rang out into the bluebook-covered classroom. "Pencils down."

Despite heinous karma swirling over my school, the gods did smile on me in terms of my last big academic hurdle of the semester. Maybe I was a social leper, but in the grades department I was feeling confident. I exhaled as I handed in my exam with a smile, ready to bolt home. Ahhhh, school's out! But then I felt the sting of memory: School may be over till the new year, but the Gold and Silver was the last obstacle in front of me.

Whitney and I had looked forward to the Gold and Silver for years—and here it was upon us and we weren't even talking. I didn't want to go at all, but I had bought my ticket in October and there was no backing out now after shelling out the *two-fitty*, which was my early Sweet Sixteen present from my parents. Whit and I always said we'd get our hair done together, get mani/pedis, and do frock auditions, but now I had to get dressed solo.

I had spied a Carolina Herrera gown in a Madison Avenue boutique window a month before, and in my head I'd done a variation for my gown—long and white with thin straps, very elegant and simple but pure glamour. Since I wasn't having my own big bash, this would be my special gown of the year, and I'd been in various stages of sketching, cutting, and sewing for weeks. When I finally put it on, the clouds above my head started to part. It was more beautiful than I'd ever expected. My mom came in to fasten the fabric-covered buttons into the silk loops I'd made (very couture, no zippers here!), and I took a big gulp and kissed my parents good-bye.

Like Cinderella I had a golden chariot—a New York taxicab. When it pulled up in front of the hotel next to all the limos, I stepped out holding my huge white silk and tulle skirt and walked into the grand lobby, past the older girls smoking cigarettes and tuxedo-clad guys taking not-so-secret swigs from sterling monogrammed flasks. I had arranged to meet Kaitlin in the lobby so we could enter together. She would normally be hanging with Sophie, but apparently Sophie's parents were dropping her off on their way back from a "small party at Calvin Klein's house" and Sophie wasn't sure exactly when she'd hit the ball. Since Kaitlin didn't want to enter solo, she remembered that I was still her friend and called me to arrange a rendezvous. That was one thing that was annoying about Ava and Kaitlin. It's like, it wasn't *their* fight, and yet they had also drifted away from me.

They were totally friendly, but they were so scared of Sophie and Whitney that it was almost like they had to hide that we were friends. It was lame, and when Kaitlin had asked me to meet her, I had called her out on it and she fully fessed up. We semi-patched things up and planned to hang more in the future.

Walking into the ball was a little surreal. It definitely had the vibe of an older party. I suddenly felt thrust into a more grown-up soiree where the stakes (and sins) were higher, the kids faster, the scene more intimidating. Walking down the long carpeted hallway, it was very *Pretty in Pink*, except *my* dress rocked. But I had the same Ringwaldian insecurity and wave of stress.

Max immediately approached us and put his arm around Kaitlin. I glanced around the hall to see who else had arrived. Just then I saw Sophie, who was in a floor-length pale pink sexy plunging Versace dress. She ran over giddily, as if her five-inch Manolos were Keds, and embraced Kaitlin and Max as I looked on from the sidelines. It was so immature; I was standing right there, but she acted like I was invisible. I walked away from the group and left them all chatting about Sophie's *amazing* time at Calvin's. They just seemed so shallow and petty at that moment that I didn't want to be near them. As I was moving toward the door Kaitlin shot me a look and started to come over, but I just waved her away. Let them hang out. I didn't need them.

Just before I entered one of the doors that led into the twinkling ballroom, I spied Whitney and Ava coming out of another door, whispering. I could immediately tell that Whit had something up her sleeve. Maybe coming tonight was a big mistake. I had a bad feeling that serious stuff was about to go down.

I walked around the ballroom, pretending to look for friends but feeling very alone. It was such a glamorous party, with dozens of flowers and a full orchestra, and it would have been so much fun to be there with friends. I wondered now why I had even come. I felt like such a loser as I stood off to the side, taking it all in.

"Hey, Laura, lookin' foxy," said Josh, who had slinked up alongside me.

"Oh," I said, startled."Hi, Josh."

"Dude, I am fully hammered. We started getting sloshed at Bobby's at, like, three o'clock."

Great. Like I cared.

"So, Laura, want some?" Josh held up a thermos and teetered back and forth so much that I thought I would get motion sickness. I politely excused myself to the bathroom to get away from him.

I stood in the stall for five minutes. I had never wanted to push the fast-forward button more on an evening. Before unlocking my stall to exit, I heard two girls enter, laughing.

"So you know that girl Whitney from my club?" asked one.

"Whitney Blake, right? From Tate?" said the other.

"Yeah. So she said she's fully about to pull this crazy historic prank on some bitch everyone hates at her school, so we have to hurry!"

"Oh my God, totally, lemme just put some more Lip Venom on. I need to look extra pouty and Angelina-ish if I'm gonna mack with Coke Saunders. He's back from Choate and he looks *hot.*"

"Tell me about it. Okay, you look properly collagenized. Let's sprint."

My heart fell. Holy moly, what was Whitney planning?

I went out into the throngs of people and looked around for someone—anyone—who was a friend I could turn to. It was one thing to be frozen out in the Tate hallways; that was local warfare. But to amp it up in public, in front of all the schools, upper-classmen, and guys, that was overboard.

The crowded massive ballroom was loud with the buzz of music, chatter, and laughter. No one looked familiar to me. I spotted a bunch of Chapin girls I'd seen at a field hockey game, but no one I really knew. Then, across the room, I saw Whitney whispering to Josh and two guys I didn't know. All were passing around Josh's thermos with God knows what concoction in it. I wondered where Jake was—I remembered him mentioning that his family wasn't leaving for vacation 'til the next day.

This was ridiculous. I decided now was as good a time as any to confront Whitney and stop all of this immature behavior, including whatever she had up her design sleeve for tonight. On my way over, I was practically knocked down by throngs of designer-clad, dewy-skinned beauties and their loosened-bow-tie escorts. Just as I approached Whitney, I saw her eyes widen, and she looked to her right, where Sophie was standing at the bar.

"Whitney," I said, stopping right in front of her. "What's going on? I just heard—"

"Laura, get out of the way," Whitney said, looking worried.

"Why? Are you planning—"

"No, not her!" Whitney screamed, seemingly to someone behind me.

Bam. A guy with a giant brown paper bag on his head flew up right behind me, grabbed my butt and squeezed, and ran off. I whipped around and saw him running away through the gilded doors, laughing. And then I saw the wide-eyed party guests staring at me.

I looked down at the back of my ivory dress, which was now glistening with red paint. My stunning gown that I had labored over now looked like I had a full period attack all over it, like the heavy-bleeding *Godfather* days, as Whitney called them, 'cause of all the gore in the movie. I felt dizzy. I turned to look at Whitney, who looked mortified. Between a spell of gasps, laughter, *"Holy shit"*s, and *"Sweet Jesus"*s from the chaperones, I fainted.

When I slowly came back into consciousness a few seconds later, I was lying on the ground faceup. The conductor from the band was fanning me, and both Whitney and Sophie were looking down at me. And between them was Jake.

Move over, Olympic sprinters. Move over, gazelles: Legs have never moved faster. Before I could even process what had just happened to me, I was running through the lobby, trying desperately to get outside.

"Laura, wait!" I heard Jake yell. At the sound of his voice, the rocket within me spurred my feet into a literal sprint, and within seconds I was through the revolving door, into the winter air, slamming a cab door behind me, and as the car screeched away, my worn-out body bent over in shaking sobs.

Chapter Twenty-five

After being calmed down by my parents, who were distraught to find me home so quickly, not to mention with a butt coated in red paint, I boiled myself in the bathtub. I wanted to wash away not just the paint, which had seeped through my dress and onto my legs and glutes, but I also wanted to wash away all the recent events. Cleanse the hatred, cleanse the meanness, cleanse the immaturity out of my life. I wanted to beam myself to adulthood, where this BS was a thing of the past, where evil girls and competition and this rat race were finished.

But would they ever be? I could be taking sad, foamy baths like this forever, moments where I would wish my troubles could pop away like the glistening bubbles and my stress would dissolve like a sliver of soap lost at the bottom of the tub.

My depressing porcelain prayer ground was suddenly invaded, however, when I heard the buzzer ring. I heard my mom talking into the speaker and knew we had visitors. Ugh. I pulled the plug on the bath and on my hopes for a quiet recovery and put on my bathrobe. When I came out, hair still wet and face still damp from both bathwater and tears, I found Kaitlin and Ava, equally dewy in my living room.

They were both crying. I hadn't seen them together in the same room since the war broke out, but through my blurred vision and stuttered speech I managed to ask them what they were doing there. They gushed apologetic sobs.

"Laura, I'm so, so sorry you ended up in the middle. You were the only sane one," Ava said, convulsively crying.

"I can't believe all this crap," said Kaitlin, wiping her eyes. "I'm sorry for being such a freak lately, I don't know what I was thinking." She wept. "I feel awful that I participated in Sophie's retarded vendettas."

"Me, too, with Whit's," said Ava. "I never meant for this to happen. Whit and Sophie are mortified, too."

For some reason that didn't make me feel better. I nodded and tried to force a grateful smile for their visit, but their apologies did little to ease the sick feeling in the pit of my stomach.

Then, to make matters worse, the loud buzzer rang again. I groaned. Great, a free-for-all. Whitney came running in, totally red-faced and crying, in her full Marie Antoinette–style gown, followed by Sophie, with the same tortured look, but in a beaded slipdress.

"Laura!" screamed Whitney, running up to hug me. I stood perfectly still.

"Laura, we're sorry!" cried Sophie.

I was too traumatized to even speak. Just seeing them in my living room after the crushing heinosity they'd put me through was too much.

"Laura! Please listen to us!" Whitney sobbed.

"What?" I shouted, the loudness of my voice surprising even me. "What do you want from me?!"

"I'm so sorry!" Whitney cried. "I didn't mean for it to get on you—"

"Yeah, it was meant for me, you psycho—" Sophie screamed at Whitney.

"You bitch, just leave me alone with my best friend," Whitney yelled back. "This is just as much your fault as mine! *Get out!*"

"I'm apologizing!" said Sophie, now crying harder than Whitney. "I never meant to hurt you, Laura!"

I saw my parents peering in from the kitchen. They hadn't seen drama like this since their opera subscription had lapsed. It was quite a scene and a half. There I was, looking like a drowned rat, with four sobbing girls, dressed in full gowns and streaming

Maybelline, all gathered around me. It was the same gang as always, but rife with wars and rage and hurt feelings. Especially mine.

I took a deep breath. "You two are disgusting. You have been so pathetic and I've really seen your true colors—and they are worse than teal, salmon, and puce. You sicken me."

"It was an accident—" Sophie sobbed, begging me to listen, but I ignored her.

"Whitney," I said, looking in her eyes. "I've been your best friend for ten years, and it only took you ten minutes to turn on me and say horrible things. And you, Sophie. I honestly don't know what I saw in you. Please both leave." They stood there, stunned and quietly whimpering. "Okay," I continued. "If you won't get out, I will." I turned and walked into my room, closed the door, and bawled into my pillow.

Chapter Twenty-six

There wasn't really a silver lining in sight for the monster storm cloud that had torrentially poured on my sophomore year so far, but hey, at least I was on Christmas break for three weeks. I had never needed it so badly. I stayed in bed and convalesced the first few days. I really truly fell ill from all the horror at school. My mom or dad would come in every now and then and report a phone call from Sophie or Whitney, but I wouldn't take their calls. They each dispatched Kaitlin and Ava to come see me—they were scared of my inner wrath that had recently been released—but Ava and Kaitlin were really unable to make any sort of case for Sophie and Whitney and admitted they wanted the whole thing to be over also. It was a pretty gloomy time, especially with the white snow turning into dirty slush outside and an angry chill gripping the city.

On the fourth day, I lay in bed halfheartedly sketching some new dress designs—I'd been unable to salvage my paint-saturated gown and hoped a new dress would take my mind off of it—when my mom knocked on my door and came in.

"Whitney called again," she said, sitting on the edge of my bed.

"I'm not talking to her."

"She just wants you to know that she's leaving tonight for Barbados or the Bahamas, hmm . . . I can't remember which one, the Bahamas, I think? Anyway, she'll call you when she's back."

"Great. Whatever. She can call, but I won't talk to her."

"I don't blame you," said my mom, pushing a strand of my hair behind my ear.

"Mom, why is high school the melting pot of evil?" I asked.

My mom clasped her hands and looked up at the ceiling, concentrating. My parents always took my questions seriously and never just whipped out a flippant answer.

"You want to know my theory?" she asked finally. "I think it's because teenagers don't get enough cuddling. Children get lots of hugs and kisses, and adults in romantic relationships do as well. But teenagers . . . they're a little tactophobic. They just don't like to be touched. They're not used to it. A hug can be a terrific emotional balm."

Hmm. "That's a good point. I mean, we don't go around hugging girls, and if we go around hugging boys we get a reputation, and if we hug our parents, we're losers. I think you may be onto something, Mom."

"So can I give you a hug?" she asked, smiling.

"Sure."

We hugged for a really long time. I'm sure my ex-friends would say it was dumb, but I didn't care.

"Don't worry about me, Mom. I'll be okay."

"Oh, I'm not worried about you," she said, rising. "I'm never worried about you. You're armed with all the good qualities necessary to take on the world, Laura. That's something that privilege can't buy."

God, I loved my parents. And that was something Sophie and Whitney definitely could not say.

The next three weeks were a perfect example of all those weird New Agey experiences that Dr. Phil and Oprah extol. I had free time to "regroup" and "recover" and "reconnect with my inner self." All that psychobabble can actually be somewhat truthful, because it is healing to just hang out alone and focus on yourself. Sophie had left a message that she was jetting off to Aspen but would check in when she got back. Like I cared. With Sophie and Whitney away skiing and sunning, I tried to forget about them, and fully immersed myself in Lower Manhattan. I didn't go uptown once, which is probably why I was able to escape and not think at all about the birthday party drama.

I actually spent almost the entire time concentrating on my designs. I thought a lot about what Whitney had said about me borrowing her stuff, and I realized I didn't need or want to borrow her clothes or accessories anymore. Don't get me wrong; they were beautiful, and I hoped one day I would be able to own my own Chloé gown, but I had faith in my designs and knew if I got back to work, I could make dresses that were just as good.

I spent weeks wandering through NoLita, the Lower East Side, and Williamsburg, taking notes at my favorite stores and hanging out in Incubator, watching Jade in action. She was cool and showed me her sketchbooks and tear sheets and told me what she thought would be the big trends for spring. I also went to Chinatown and scanned the fabrics, looking for ideas, and visited button stores and ribbon warehouses. No petite nook in the Garment District was too little for me. I had never felt so creatively engaged, and it was such a nice feeling. I realized I had wasted too much time on those stupid parties and catfights, and my New Year's resolution was to try not to give a damn and stay true to myself.

My one source of anxiety was Jake. I mean, I had been a little nasty to him and I felt bad. I was just tired of the way he was taking his time choosing between Sophie and Whitney and really wished he would get on with it so he would put us all out of our misery. I mean, they call me Switzerland and tell *me* to choose or lose? If I was Switzerland, then he was Geneva. He's the capital of Waffler Land. I guess he chose Sophie when he kissed her. But why did he still act like he wasn't with her, and why did he seem confused when I mentioned her that day at the bus stop? The bottom line was that it was none of my business, so I really shouldn't have been rude. I tried to ignore it and on Christmas even prayed a little in church that I didn't hurt his feelings. (I am sooo dorky, I know.) I also felt a little weird that he'd witnessed the humiliating debacle that was the Gold and Silver Ball—and that he hadn't called me. I guess after my harsh treatment of him that day at the bus stop, our friendship really was over. I also closet-repented for the one deadly sin that was creeping its way into my conscience, no matter how hard I tried to stuff it back down: Envy. I was Kermit-green with envy about that spin the bottle night. I had to admit it to myself finally: I liked Jake. A lot. All this time, I felt delusional—how could he ever be into me when two of the most gorge gals at Tate were fighting over him? Then I started thinking, But he calls me, we're better friends, and isn't that the most important thing? I screwed it all up by going psycho on him. So my holiday was tainted with regret, but then, on New Year's Eve, I got my belated Christmas present.

I was sitting at home, watching the ball drop with my parents, when the phone rang.

"Hey, Finnegan . . ."

It was Jake.

"I hope I'm not calling too late—I assumed you'd be up ringing in the New Year," he continued.

"Hey, Jake! I'm just at home having a Dick Clark fest with my 'rents. How's Antigua?" I asked, trying not to show I was excited.

"Great. You know, sunny every day, nothing special. I just . . . wanted to say hey."

"I'm so glad you called." I wasn't sure what to say about my snappage at him the last time we spoke, and I didn't even want to bring up the night of the ball. "Um . . . Jake, sorry I was such a stress case last time I talked to you. I was having a total coronary."

"No problem. I hope things are better."

"Yeah, things are better now. Hey, the ball's dropping! So weird that we sit here every year and, like, half the world watches this little ball drop. What is the meaning behind that, would someone tell me?"

Jake laughed. "I don't know, but you are so observant."

"It's just weird, right?"

"Okay, Dad!" Jake said, his voice muffled. I guess he was being summoned. "Listen, I have to bolt; the fam's waiting for me. But I just wanted to say Happy New Year, Laura. It's going to be a great year."

"You think so?" I asked, hopeful.

"Definitely. I feel it in my bones."

"I hope you're right. Happy New Year, Jake."

"See you soon, Finnegan."

When I hung up, my parents looked at me curiously. I turned deep red. "What?"

"Nothing," they replied in unison, smiling. Then they gave each other a look. But I didn't care. I was thrilled. I hoped he was right about it being a great year. That made my day.

Chapter Twenty-seven

After buying fabric, gathering grosgrain samples, and spending time sketching galore from the comfort of my cocoon—I mean, bedroom—I decided to turn the pages and pages of on-paper dresses into 3-D. I swear, I did not move my ass from my sewing station for fourteen hours. For three days, my parents poked their heads in, asking if they could bring me food or water, like I was going on some Mahatma Gandhi hunger strike. But it wasn't a political statement; it was almost a statement to myself—that I could do it, that I had the goods, and that I didn't need Whitney's intro to Oscar or Sophie's to Calvin. I was officially taking the plunge and going from designing my own duds to amping it up a notch and attempting what I never even had the guts to dream about: my own line. For some reason, hitting rock bottom thrust me into a little universe of my own, and my solitude turned into strength, which turned into a way out of the black hole. I started to think, as I looked in my closet, if D&G or LV can be hot, why not LF? By the end of my stitching rampage, I had sixteen kick-ass pieces—a cool A-line skirt with leather ribbon piping, a pintucked blouse, a swirl-skirted strapless dress, and a bunch of cami tops and cowl-neck knits. With my heart beating, I packed them into one of my dad's old L.L. Bean navy duffels and left the house before I lost my nerve.

"Whoa, girlie!" Jade beamed as my cheeks flushed with elation. "These are *ferocious*!"

I had mustered every ounce of courage I had and brought my designs to Incubator to find out if I had the goods from my fashion god, Jade. I was unprepared for her reaction, especially since she was the queen of low affect. But she held up each of my pieces, surveying the cuts and details, and smiled over and over again. "Laura, I'm dying! These cap-sleeved blouses are so well tailored!"

"Thanks . . . ," I said meekly. I was so nervous and excited—this was my fashion idol talking and I was semi in shock. She confirmed that my hermetic sewfest had been worth it.

"I think I have a design prodigy on my hands," she marveled. "I can't believe you're only sixteen!"

"Almost." I smiled. "I'm technically fifteen for twenty-four more hours."

As she went on and on, I became more and more proud. It was amazing to be validated, and awesome to be praised for doing something that I worshiped.

January 4, the last night of Christmas break before school started again, was my birthday. My Sweet Sixteen. I hadn't reminded anyone and didn't even send out invitations, because I knew no one would show except Kaitlin and Ava, who had called me repeatedly over the vaycay from their respective beach resorts to check in. It was finally dawning on me how surreal it was that my ex–best friend of a decade, Whitney, wasn't coming. Nor was Sophie. Even though they were both racked with guilt, they were now semi-scared of me, so they wouldn't dare to show up. Not that I was bummed, since both of them had been such monsters. We had our little votive-lit glistening table in the corner at Chez Michel, and my mom ordered some apps for the little but loving group.

"What else would you girls like?" my dad asked.

"The bruschetta looks amazing," said Ava, her mouth watering.

"Ooh, and that onion tartlet," gushed Kaitlin, looking at the neighboring table in the bustling restaurant.

"Laura?" my mom probed.

I was in the zone. "Oh, whatever you guys want . . ." Busted. I had been staring off into space. Well, not space, exactly. As I'd heard the waiter drone on with the interminable list o' specials, I looked around the small restaurant. A hot guy squeezing his model girlfriend's hand in one corner. A cute yummy mummy and her gorge husband with their sophisticated child at another. A kiss here, a hand hold there. I sighed. My sixteenth b-day wasn't turning out so sweet.

"Oh my God," Kaitlin said, shattering my reverie. "Laura, do I have goss for you! Okay, guess what? Sophie *flipped* on her mom last night!"

"What?" I asked, actually sort of curious.

"Yeah, she basically called her out on all her sh—" She stopped, looking at my parents. "—on all her bad behavior."

According to Kaitlin, Sophie had confessed to her mom that she was feeling really bad about the way she treated me, and rather than take the high road, as parents are supposed to (right?), her mom told her she was a spineless fool and to get a life. Then Sophie bitched out her mom and told her she was a social-climbing loser who lived in a friendless universe and she wanted nothing to do with her.

When Kaitlin finished telling her story, even my parents were shocked.

"No way!" I said, in awe.

"Way," replied Kaitlin, eyes ablaze.

"I don't believe this!" said Ava, stunned.

"Why not? Sophie has guts, we knew that," said Kaitlin.

"No, no, not that," said Ava. "I'm shocked because Whitney did the exact same thing this morning!"

"What?" we all asked.

Yes, it was true. Whitney had told her mom that she was dreading going back to school and felt bad about me, and about Sophie, and her mom told her she was pathetic, and Whitney just lost it. She finally stood up to her mom (about time, in my opinion) and told her she was cruel and critical and that she could never please her and—according to Ava—told her mom that "Laura was a better person than she would ever be"!

Whoa. I never thought Whitney would ever stand up to her mother. I was impressed.

Ava looked at me earnestly. "She really feels bad about everything, Laura."

"So does Sophie," added Kaitlin.

"Wow," I said, feeling slightly more forgiving toward my two torturers. "Good for them."

I was glad they were feeling remorse. I hoped they would grow up and stop all this nonsense, and it looked like they might finally be on the right course. But if Whitney and Sophie's sudden chutzpah in my defense was the dawn of a happy new year (for the calendar and my life), the next thing I beheld was an even better forecast: stunning blush pink peonies placed in front of me. I looked up, instantly feeling my cheeks match the hue of the buds.

"Happy birthday, Finnegan," Jake said, tan and smiling. "Sorry I'm late."

Chapter Twenty-eight

It turns out Jake had called again over Christmas break and asked my parents how I was doing, in addition to calling on New Year's Eve. They had weirdly struck up some sort of parental friendship with Jake and had invited him, unbeknownst to me. And when he sat down at the table after greeting everyone hello, I felt a flush of pride and . . . I don't know . . . well, love wash over me. I mean, the guy was *gorgeous* and like the most sought-after dude in the city, and he had come to *my* birthday. *My* birthday! He didn't care that Sophie and Whitney had discarded me and declared me a loser. He didn't care that it wasn't at a million-dollar venue. My party had no frills, no fancy dresses, no lights, and no music except for the harmonized voices of three starving actors slash waiters singing "Happy Birthday."

After Jake's arrival, I suddenly felt like I was glowing in the flickering candlelight, and I was so happy looking around at my friends and family sitting at our cozy little table on this snowy night. His presence made everything seem right. In the middle of random conversations, like when Ava was telling us about her ski instructor in Sun Valley or Kaitlin was talking about the new Four Seasons in Hawaii, Jake would catch my eye and smile, and I felt this weird warmth. Sixteenth birthdays didn't come sweeter.

After putting Ava and Kaitlin in a cab uptown, my mom and dad announced they were heading home to catch *Charlie Rose*. I was about to go with them and bid farewell to my crush when Jake asked me to go for a walk with him. Before I could even respond, my parents fled, telling us to have a good time. I think they wanted me to be with Jake even more than I did. Not possible.

"Thanks again for my present," I said, looking down at the beautiful and chic Tiffany gold-link bracelet that Jake had given me. It had a little gold charm on it—a goldfish—to commemorate our visit to the kois by the Met.

"I thought you should have a pet goldfish. Plus, this guy has a longer memory than twelve seconds."

I laughed. "I love it so much," I said, staring into Jake's beautiful eyes.

We crunched along the snowy sidewalk, weaving our way down the little streets that make up the West Village. The snow had silenced the cars, and the frosty weather had kept most people at home, so it felt like we had the city to ourselves. It was just . . . magical.

"So how do you feel? Older?" asked Jake, cocking his head to the side. I loved how he never asked rhetorical questions but always wanted an answer, just like my parents.

"Oh . . . pretty much the same."

"Well, I think you kicked it off right. That was a really good time."

"Thanks for coming. I mean, I know it wasn't a full-on bash like Whitney's or Sophie's will be—"

"Laura," he said, coming to an abrupt stop and putting his hand on my shoulder. "It was better."

"Oh, thanks, but I know they're like—"

Again Jake interrupted. "Laura, I don't care about Sophie or Whitney. I never have." He looked at me with a sly smile and I thought I'd break into a fever. "I care about you."

I was so stunned that I sputtered my response. "But—but—but, what about making out with Sophie in the closet?"

Jake looked surprised. "What? I blew her off. I told her I wasn't into her, and she accused me of liking Whitney, and I told her I wasn't into her either."

No way. Oh joy, oh joy, oh joy! "Really?" My beaming face bespoke my utter elation and over-the-moon uncontainable euphoria.

"Finnegan, don't you get it? I call *you*. I only go to parties if *you* are there. Those girls mean nothing to me, and they should mean nothing to you because you are so much better than them," he said, coming closer to me and taking my hand. "You're smarter, you're prettier, you're funnier, and your party, I guarantee you, was a whole lot better than theirs will be. You have something they don't have. You have a soul. And you shouldn't waste your time comparing yourself to them, because there's no comparison. You're it."

And before I could respond, Jake—the normally cool cat—pulled me into his arms and started kissing me.

There are no words. Zilch. Okay, fine, one: heaven.

I was *in* heaven. I felt his hand slide down my back and protectively clasp me, pulling me closer to him. It may have been two degrees outside, but in his arms I felt like I was on fire. And for the first time ever, I threw myself into the flames without fear of getting burned.

When we finally stopped kissing, Jake took me by the hand and led me up the street.

"I want to show you something," he said, and I followed, giddily.

He stopped in front of a beautiful brick town house with black shutters and now-frozen window boxes for flowers. He took out a key and led me up the stairs.

"Jake, whose house is this?"

"I'm just breaking in," he replied, smiling.

"Seriously."

"It's my dad's architect's place. Come on. He's away, so we have it to ourselves."

Jake unlocked the door and ushered me inside the beautifully restored entrance. He grabbed my hand, and we walked up the sweeping mahogany staircase until we reached the tippy top. He opened French doors that led outside to the roof, and when I walked out, I couldn't believe my eyes.

The skyscrapers in the distance were ablaze with light. I looked around and suddenly stopped in my tracks. The roof looked out on the Chrysler Building. Little Christmas-tree lights were strewn along the planted trees, and my eyes followed the longest extension cord I'd ever seen to a small record player on a low table. It looked exactly like the poster in my room that Jake had admired. He'd remembered.

"My God, Jake, it's just like the poster!" I gasped.

"Not until we do this," said Jake, walking over to the record player. He turned it on and an old song by Stevie Wonder came on, "I Believe." He took my hand, wrapped his other arm around me, and we started to dance. I was dancing with Jake Watkins in the rooftop of my dreams. Oh. My. God.

"This is so surreal," I said, dizzy with joy. "I can't believe you'd do this for me."

"Why wouldn't I?"

"I don't know . . . why would you?" I said, looking straight into his piercing green eyes.

"Because, Finnegan, I just love . . . your . . . way."

And then we kissed, the most amazing kiss of my life. I was living the grainy, sublime, simple wish that had floated above my dreaming head since I was a child. And I never wanted to wake up.

Chapter Twenty-nine

With the lilting sound track of Jake's post-dinner evening carrying me through the air, the next morning I felt like my daily grind of a commute was a soothing magic carpet ride. The usual subway din was suddenly music, the stench of the packed car felt perfumed, and even the muffin that I picked up at the corner deli by Tate tasted like it was baked from scratch by a four-star chef. Life was good. My last day at Tate had been marred with humiliation from hell, and I now felt like a cupid-shot cloud niner. And that was all the armor I needed.

As I filled my hot chocolate at the morning coffee bar, Whitney approached me. Honestly, maybe I got a little jolt of nervousness, but it was nothing compared to what it would have been sans lovefest with Jake. I truly felt like what happened between us shielded me from all the unpleasant chaos that led up to Christmas break.

"Laura, I know you hate me," she started. I didn't say anything. I wasn't sure I hated her, but I sure didn't like her right now. "I would hate me, too. You have every single right to loathe me. What I did to you was . . . horrible."

I stared at her. I was glad that she was apologizing, but I didn't want to let her off so easily. She had let me down, to say the least.

"You've been my best friend for so long," she continued. "And I miss you so much."

"It really took you a long time to realize that," I said.

"I know, I know. I became everything that I always swore I wouldn't. I acted like my mother. I am so ashamed."

Whitney burst into tears. It was weird, because in all our years of friendship, I had rarely seen her cry. And this time it wasn't a few crocodile tears for show—her body actually started convulsing and shaking with sobs.

I felt sad for her all of a sudden. She seemed so genuinely devastated, that was clear. But my hurt feelings resurfaced—she had been so quick to drop me for Sophie, and then even quicker to freeze me out when I didn't immediately go back with her like a puppy. "Whitney, you were . . . so unbelievably nasty to me" was all I could say.

Her sobs grew in response—I think she knew how right I was. "What can I do to make it up to you? I am so sorry."

"You're *sorry*? Sorry about which part? That you were psycho to me for weeks? That you got so wrapped up in your Sweet Sixteen party that you were ready to flush our friendship down the toilet?"

"I was wrong." Whitney bawled. "I love you. I'd cancel my whole dumb party if you wanted me to. Just say the word."

I exhaled slowly. It was too tough giving it to someone in tears, even though revenge had been on my mind since I'd been ambushed with faux period stains. As I was wondering what Whit could possibly do to make it up to me, Sophie came up, also red-faced.

"Laura, I am so, so mortified by the way I acted." She sniffed. "I was just jealous of your friendship with Whitney. I wanted to fit in. I really messed everything up. . . ."

I didn't protest.

She continued. "I feel like I'm the girl who came in and ruined everything," she said, crying harder. "I never meant for all this to happen."

"Then why did you let it happen?" I asked archly.

Sophie was about to say something to defend herself but stopped. "I don't know. There's no excuse," she admitted.

"You really hurt my feelings. I was trying to help you both. *I* was the peacemaker, and you turned on me," I said.

"I'm sorry," they both murmured in unison.

"And even before that, you both went off the deep end," I said, very calmly. "Don't you see now that it takes so much energy to hate someone? Doesn't it wrench your guts and haunt your soul morning, noon, and night? Hate is so all-consuming, I can't believe you guys didn't pass out from exhaustion!"

"I almost did," admitted Sophie.

"Me, too," said Whitney, looking at Sophie. It was the first utterance they'd made to each other that wasn't dipped in arsenic. "I haven't slept in weeks."

"Me neither," said Sophie, looking back at Whitney.

"You both were so incredibly mean. Just mean."

Whitney and Sophie started crying harder after hearing my pronouncement. Mean. They knew it wasn't as haughty as "bitchy" or cool as "rude" or pointed as "snide." Just *mean*. Like children.

"I know. And I'm so sorry," said Whitney.

"Me, too," said Sophie.

"Okay, then," I said. "If you're really sorry and you really want to make it up to me, then you two have to make up with each other. I can't deal with another semester of war zones."

Sophie and Whitney paused and looked at each other. Then at the floor.

"What's the problem, guys? Haven't you had enough?"

Silence. Finally, Whitney broke the twenty hockey rinks

full of ice. "Yes, I've had enough," Whitney said. "I'm sorry, Sophie."

Sophie upped the ante with—gasp!—a hug, which even Whit didn't seem ready for. "I'm sorry, too!" she cried, embracing Whitney and then engulfing me into the hug. We stepped back, all reeling from the developments. I felt like doves were gonna come flying out and a full purple-robed choir singing "Hallelujah!" would be revealed behind a curtain.

"Not to defer the blame," started Sophie, looking at us seriously. "But my mom totally goaded me on. I really never wanted to hurt you. Either of you. I can't believe I was such a fool to listen to her."

"My mom was involved, too," said Whitney conspiratorially. "She egged me on the whole time." She paused and looked at me. "And I do not want to end up like my mother."

"Me neither," said Sophie. "I was scared I was becoming her for a while there."

"Me too!" Whitney laughed. "It was horrifying."

I smiled to see flickers of the old warmth starting to come back. I knew it would take a little while for the thaw. But at least the match was lit. The bell rang for class and our newly cobbled-together triumvirate had to part ways.

"Hey, Laura," Whitney said as I gathered my bag. "Ava told me about Jake. I am really happy for you. I think you're a great couple, and I mean that honestly."

"Thanks, Whit." I smiled.

"Yeah, I had a feeling my Jake crush was a lost cause," Sophie confessed. "I think he was smitten with you from the get-go."

I guess everyone knew it but me. Better to be last to know, though, I thought. It made it that much sweeter.

Chapter Thirty

Little by little the darkness subsided, and the gap was bridged. Whitney and Sophie were totally enthusiastic about my new designs and flipped out when I told them that Jade had agreed to sell them at Incubator. Sophie had us all laughing about what a fool she made of herself in front of Don Johnson's son in Aspen, and Whitney told us about another lifeguard she'd met. As the icicles cracked off our frozen friendship, the freeze that had overtaken our lives melted away and was replaced by hilarious fun. It seemed almost like old times.

On the birthday party front, Whitney and Sophie had decided to still proceed as planned with separate parties. But luckily, they were totally supportive of each other, and all our friends and classmates agreed to stop by both. Thank God the Plaza and the Pierre are so close to each other!

I flipped a coin to see whose party I would go to first and came up with Whitney's. Sophie was totally cool with that, and I planned on being at her bash at nine. The only bummer of the whole sitch was that Jake categorically refused to attend either party on principle. At first I tried to persuade him, but then I decided to respect his wishes. Ultimately I decided it was kind of hot that he was not into the whole party thing. I always think it's a little nerdy when a guy is way into some girly soiree, and I liked that my man could take it or leave it. He did agree to pick me up at eleven and we were going to get pizza. So I was left to make my way to the parties solo, which was fine, because I planned to be very zen about the whole thing.

There was so much pressure on these parties to bc the best ever that even the tabloids got involved. The *New York Post* started running headlines over how much they cost and who was attending which. *Teen Vogue* had asked for an exclusive on Whitney's, and *In Style* would cover Sophie's if the promised celebrities attended. That sent all the girls into a frenzy. Madison Avenue had never seen so much business from fifteen- and sixteen-year-olds. Tailors worked overtime. The best hair and makeup people in the city were booked. I even heard that Tom

Ford came out of retirement to help one girl with her dress. It was major.

Finally, January 28 rolled around—the big day had arrived. The parties were about to be launched in full force. There was a flurry of phone calls all day reporting Mary Hart spottings. It was all craziness. And I heard from one witness who happened to walk past 59th Street that there were so many burly men seen hauling lights and sets into the hotels that it looked like they were setting up for a Broadway musical in the Pierre and a Vegas show in the Plaza. As girls all over New York prepped—laying out gowns, waxing their legs, crimping their hair, spritzing perfumes, polishing their nails, and making last-minute panty hose purchases, I took a deep breath and had a preparty snack with my parents.

I had made my own gown for the evening, inspired by Phoebe Philo of Chloé, which was a light blue chiffon column dress with a black velvet bow-belt. It had taken a long, long time, but I was proud of it, and when I had shown it to Jake the weekend before he had pronounced it "smokin'," which made me super psyched.

"Honey, have a great, great time," said my mom and dad as they put me into a cab.

They had thrown on coats over their pajamas and come down to see me off. (It was only seven o'clock, but they liked to be cozy.)

My parents stood there beaming as if I were off to my first prom. (In fact, they had taken my picture several times. And sweet Jake had even sent me a corsage—kind of a joke, but a flower nonetheless.)

"Okay, guys, gotta go," I said, rolling up the window. "Love you!"

The cab pulled away, crunching over the packed snow. I looked at my parents out the back window as they smiled and waved. I bet that Sophie's and Whitney's parents never walked them outside or saw them off for anything. And that made me a little sad. I waved again as we turned the corner. I may have been going to my best friends' parties, which were going to be the most expensive Sweet Sixteen bashes that New York had ever seen, but I truly felt like the lucky one.

Chapter Thirty-one

The gilded, carved double doors of the Pierre ballroom burst open to the mixing sounds of Peter Duchin's famed orchestra, gales of laughter, and clinking crystal champagne flutes. I scanned the scene, and boy was it ever a scene. Palm trees lined the entire ballroom and dance floor like I had been beamed to Florida, *Star Trek* style. It was insanity. After months and months of planning, it was so amazing to see all of the ideas come to life. And everything was more glamorous and elaborate than I could have imagined.

Waiters in seersucker suits passed out tropical drinks with freshly cut orchids, and custom daiquiri stands were placed strategically as the bartenders poured their concoctions into giant conch shells. David Copperfield performed his tricks on a stage covered with pink sand imported from Bermuda, and a giant glass pool filled with mermaids drew attention on another custom-built platform. The bold-faced names, the ones you read about in every society column in New York, were all in attendance. Oscar de la Renta toasted Brooke Astor, who waved a white-gloved hand to Blaine Trump, who nodded her head to Tinsley Mortimer, all as the *New York Times'* Bill Cunningham snapped away with his camera for the Sunday Styles section. Every second it seemed like another stylish fashionista fluttered by to air-kiss another jet-setter.

I waited in the seemingly endless receiving line, which snaked through the entrance like a long, silver, sequin-covered serpent of ladies in flowing frocks and gents in perfect black tie. It was so weird that this was all for Whitney. I mean, we had sat for hours in Jackson Hole Restaurant, planning and imagining what this would all be like, and now it had come to life.

When I finally got a glimpse of Whitney at the end of the line, I was stunned. She looked so beautiful. Her dress was a gorgeous strapless petal pink design, which was tight on the top but then flowed into a tulle confection. She was wearing delicate diamond chandelier earrings and a two-tiered diamond necklace that I knew were from her mother's safe-deposit box. It was all very subtle yet elegant; the whole look was reminiscent of Gwyneth's Oscar outfit. When Whitney noticed me waiting in the back of the endless receiving line, she ran past everyone and gave me a huge hug, whispering in my ear that I was the only person that she really cared to see on her birthday. She was quickly whisked away by her mother, but I was so glad she had said that.

An hour later, after shimmying under a limbo stick held by two Vilebrequin bathing-suit–wearing male models, dancing, gabbing, and checking my watch, my cue to exit rolled out on the dance floor in the form of an eleven-foot, seven-tiered cake with a replica of Whitney on top.

The agreed-upon plan was that as soon as Whit's cake came out at 9:00, I would head over to Sophie's, so I snuck to the coat check, put on my jacket, lifted my long skirt, and ran across the street from the Pierre to the Plaza.

I entered Sophie's raging shindig to find I'd left Palm Beach for the African outback. In full safari theme, every table had a different animal print, and huge, I mean, *massive*, taxidermy filled the room—stuffed elephants, giraffes, rhinos, everything. It was, like, dresses by Roberto Cavalli, flowers by Preston Bailey, decor by Discovery Channel. Male models dressed as Tarzans swung from leafy vines overhead, and zebra rugs lined the floors. Thong-clad "tribal" waiters passed shish kebabs from flaming serving trays and little rawhide tents were scattered around the room (Sophie's parents didn't know that most teens were using them for heavy-petting sessions, and I'm not talking about petting animals.) Quite literally: It was wild.

I arrived in time to see Sophie blow out the candles on her own towering cake, but just as she was about to cut into it with a shiny new Elsa Peretti sterling cake knife, an African dancer jumped out of the cake's center, startling the crowd, while a hundred African drummers entered the ballroom, dancers filed in, and Paul Simon took the stage.

There were so many people there it was hard to even get close to Sophie. After trying in vain—and getting trounced on by camera crews and sycophants—I decided to just hang out on the dance floor with Ava and Kaitlin. (They were also party-hopping.) Luckily, toward eleven o'clock, just as I was getting ready to leave and meet Jake, I was able to catch Sophie's eye across the room. She was up on the balcony, surveying the crowd with her mom, and I waved to her. She waved back and mouthed the words "I love you! Thanks for coming!" and, surprisingly, even her mom waved (giddy from the champagne, probably). But I was psyched—both Whitney and Sophie had made me feel happy for coming, and now I was off to my own private party.

I was ready. I felt like Cinderella ditching the ball to make curfew, only I wasn't running *from* my prince, I was running *to* him.

I was practically skipping down the famed Plaza steps when I saw him. Lit by the glow of the fountain in the square's center,

Jake leaned casually on the stone edge, waiting for me.

As I walked toward him, my smile growing, I thought about my net take from the evening's—and the year's—events. How weird that so much drama, anger, and anguish (not to mention millions of dollars) were spent on something that was over in a blink—like Copperfield's magic *poof!* The night had disappeared. Holding my two gift bags, one Tiffany blue, the other Cartier red, I realized I may never attend another insane over-the-top party like these in my life. And as I saw Jake get up to walk over to me, I knew that would be just fine with me.

I had changed over the last few months. I had grown stronger and become my own person. Now that Jake and I were together, I couldn't believe that I didn't see that he was into me earlier. I just didn't have the confidence to believe someone as awesome as he is could love *me*. But now I did, and it was a great lesson to have learned.

And now, as I was leaving these black-tie extravaganzas for humble pie—pizza pie, to be exact—I realized, after the past few unbelievably gut-wrenching months, that all the cheesy soft-rock ballads, fortune cookies, and cliché-packed self-help books are right: Be true to yourself and you'll be rewarded. Happiness is the best prize of all. And as Jake took me in his arms and kissed me passionately, I knew I had won the blue ribbon. The fact is, the best parties don't have a guest list of two thousand or two hundred. They have a guest list of two.

Bittersweet Sixteen

Meet Jill and Carrie!

Plan your own Sweet Sixteen bash!

Sneak peek at SUMMER INTERN

EXTRAS

A conversation with Jill and Carrie

Jill Kargman and Carrie Karasyov know firsthand about the world that they wrote about in Bittersweet Sixteen. *They've done it all: from posh private schools to over-the-top parties to growing up in New York City. We sat down with them and got the scoop on, well, everything!*

Q: How did you guys meet?

JILL KARGMAN: We actually met as little kids. Our parents were friendly and so we always kinda knew who each other was but we really became buddies in boarding school.

CARRIE KARASYOV: Yes, we went to the same school and boarding school.

Q: Were you close friends in high school?

JK: Carrie was the cool, older senior and I was the new sophomore and I was so psyched when she invited me into her dorm to order pizza. She showed me the ropes and the social lay of the land, and helped me ease into boarding-school life. I would have been lost without her!

CK: Our boarding school was totally all-American, Patagonia-clad blond kids from Connecticut, and Jill and I—both brunettes in our New Yorky outfits—stood out like sore thumbs. I left school every Saturday after classes to go back to NYC for the weekend (one whole night of it) and the dean of students said that I left more than any other student in the history of our

school. Then Jill came and he said that she surpassed my record.

Q: When did you guys start writing together?

JK: We had both worked at MTV and the same magazines and started comparing notes. We were telling funny stories about psycho editors we knew and people were laughing, telling us we had to write the over-the-top anecdotes down. So we did and we've been writing together ever since.

Q: How does your writing process work?

JK: We both flush out a really detailed outline and then we get crackin' on the writing part. First, one of us will do a chapter and then e-mail it to the other.

CK: Then we are free to add whatever we want to the other's chapter, and then back and forth. By the time we go through several drafts, each part is so layered with her writing and mine that sometimes it's hard to remember who wrote what.

Q: Do you guys ever fight?

JK: No, we really never fight. Sometimes we have differences of opinion, but we trust each other and discuss it until there's clarity on what to do. But even that's kinda rare.

Q: How did you decide to start writing for teens?

JK: We grew up on teen movies and were both voracious teen readers, and we honestly feel like we're sixteen and not—*gasp!*—double that. It actually comes even more naturally to us than writing for adults!

CK: Yes. We love John Hughes movies *[Sixteen Candles, The Breakfast Club, Pretty in Pink, Some Kind of Wonderful]* and wanted to write sort of a John Hughes–type book.

Q: How did you come up with the idea for *Bittersweet Sixteen*?

JK: We saw tons of press covering the trend of these over-the-top parties and we thought, my gosh, this is a world so ripe for the picking! We totally envisioned it as a movie, so we wrote *Bittersweet Sixteen* as a screenplay, which we sold to Paramount Pictures. The good news is, we got paid, and we got into the Writers Guild. The bad news is, the exec who bought it got canned and it was never made.

CK: So we got the rights back and wrote it as a book.

Q: Were Whit, Sophie, and Laura inspired by people you know?

JK: All our characters are flickers of familiar people in our lives, but they're really composites.

CK: The goodness of each of the characters is inspired by people we know. It's much easier to write fictitious bad people and give them mean barbs than it is to write about people who make good choices. But luckily we have good examples in our friends.

Q: What did you each do for your Sweet Sixteen?

JK: Nothing. Like, seriously: no party, nada. Just a small dinner with my family. I have a summer birthday so no one would have come, anyway!

CK: My birthday is St. Patrick's Day, so there's a parade every year. It also falls on spring break. I had just returned from Barbados and went to Mr. O's, a bar that used to be on Second Avenue and that didn't card teens. In retrospect, it's pretty scandalous that I did that. Bad example!

Plan your own Sweet Sixteen! (without any Bitter whatsoever!)

IF THIS BOOK teaches anything, it's that money doesn't buy happiness, and spending a trillion smacks on your Sweet Sixteen rager certainly doesn't make your celebration any more special. The key is to have an experience that is real: true friends, yummy food (I mean do you *really* like caviar?), and memory-making time together.

Themes: If you need a theme, do something true to *you*. Don't pick Hawaii if it means nothing to you. Go with your gut instinct. Stay away from high-maintenance concepts that would require tons and tons of decorations. Picking two fave colors is nice. Keep it simple.

Favors: No need to spend money on these. Share something you dig—like something you made or your favorite chocolate—something that will serve as a reminder of the birthday gal and what she loves.

Dresses: You want to feel pretty, so clearly go with the frock that makes you feel like a million even if you don't spend that. And it doesn't have to be some designer getup. Try on a bunch of things and narrow them down to four you really love. Then, with the help of a true pal, see if you can go with the one that is most risky for you—not too flashy, maybe just outside the box. It's always fun to do something unexpected. Also, don't go with a big trend

of the *momento*. You'll want these pics forever and you don't want to look back with horrification that you sported some jagged asymmetrical hemline only because it was in for those five seconds.

Music: DJ or iPod all the way. Bands can get cheesy and expensive, so steer clear. Plus, you wanna shimmy to the real artists and not some dorky band guy, right?

Sashay down the runway with the next fabulous treat from Jill and Carrie

Summer Intern

Chapter One

It was totally surreal: There I was in the midst of a dizzying, glittering collage of designer duds being pushed around on racks by leggy black-clad editors, with a soundtrack of whirring modems, ringing phones, and French accents playing in the background. There were models on go-sees with the bookings department, who were having Polaroids snapped of their gaunt, shiny faces. There were crocodile handbags from Hermès, Valentino, Chanel, and Marc Jacobs being gathered up for a shoot of "Scaley Chic" reptilian accessories. There was an armed guard from Van Cleef & Arpels with a briefcase cuffed to his arm as he transported gems for the "Diamonds Are a Girl's Best Friend" story, and a beret-wearing photographer having a loud fight with the sittings editor about renting out the Central Park Zoo's entire polar bear sanctuary for a ten-page layout of winter's best fur coats.

I was in the frenzied offices of *Skirt* magazine—the top of the top in fashion, pop culture, and beauty; the bible for any aesthete; the cool girl's forecast for what's hot and what to wear, listen to, even eat (i.e., carbs = the devil). It was a kaleidoscopic mix of hipsters, hotties, and badasses, all yapping a mile a minute on teeny cell phones with a stress level you'd more likely expect to see at the Pentagon rather than at Hughes Publications, the mag's parent company. But in the Gehry-architected glass-and-steel offices, the buzz of calamities at deadline was deafening. Like a trunk arriving in St. Bart's with the wrong bikinis. A beauty associate screaming at a makeup artist that the tweezing for the brow story was too arched. A beeper informing a fashion director of a snag in a Missoni dress on location. Drama was all around. And I had just reported for my introductory summer intern meeting in the gleaming glass conference room. I took my place at one of the empty seats, heart pounding. A platter of baked goods and buttered bagels sat untouched as people streamed into the room.

Beside me were my two roommates for the next two months, whom I'd only briefly met earlier that morning: Gabe, a gorgeous androgynous rocker-type with cheekbones one could slash a wrist on, and Teagan, a multiple-pierced Goth gal who was still striking and beautiful despite the sharp objects protruding from her face.

Gabe and Teagan had both arrived a couple of days before me and had already paid a visit to the *Skirt* office. The accessories director had immediately taken them under his wing, filling them in on all the need-to-know gossip.

When the meeting commenced, we were each asked to introduce ourselves. For example: "Gabe Tennant. Sagittarius. Midwesterner. Hung over." My new roomie got some chuckles.

My turn was so yawnsville: Kira Parker from Philly. I'd won the internship through a fashion sketch submission contest sponsored by Cotton, one of *Skirt*'s big advertisers. I was headed to Columbia in the fall. I also blurted out that I was "psyched" to get to know the city, and the second the words came out of my mouth like in a cartoon bubble, I realized I sounded hot off the Greyhound. Oh well. When we were all done, each editor explained which department they headed up, and then Alida Jenkins, the executive editor, took the floor to describe how the intern program worked.

She was ten minutes into her speech, explaining the guidelines of what working at *Skirt* would entail, when the door to the conference room burst open. Standing on the threshold were three extremely well-dressed girls, all with different shades of stick-straight long hair (the hair of the one on the left was dark brown with caramel highlights, while the one in the middle possessed the whitest hair outside of a Scandinavian country, and the one on the right had the same honey color as Heidi Klum). They were all clutching Venti-size cups from Starbucks and appeared to have been laughing at some hilarious joke that was so amusing they couldn't stop giggling even when they noticed that the meeting was already in session.

Now me, I would have been mortified to make such a ruckus that every head in the room whipped in my direction, but these girls didn't seem at all fazed.

"Oh my gosh, Alida! Did you start without us?" asked the white blonde in the center. She suddenly looked down at her watch, which I could see from across the room was a solid gold Cartier tank with small diamonds. "Cecilia, you didn't tell me it was ten-fifteen," she said accusingly to the Heidi Klum look-alike. With that watch, who needed their friend to tell her what time it was?

"That's okay, Daphne. Come on in. We're just getting started," said Alida with a tight smile.

"Sooooo sorry, Alida," said the platinum blonde girl. She strode up to Alida and gave her an air kiss on the cheek.

Instead of sitting down, the white blonde—obviously the leader of the pack—turned to face the other ten interns who were seated in the room.

"I'm sure I missed the name game, so I'll introduce myself now. I'm Daphne Hughes, this is my second summer interning here, and I go to Brown." She looked around the room to make sure everyone was paying attention. I moved my eyes to her friends, certain that they would now take the stage, but before they could, Daphne continued. "Listen, I just want to say that I know you all are probably really nervous right now, but don't worry. Everyone is *really* sweet here, and that's why it's the best magazine on the planet, so don't stress. Of course, they'll work us hard, won't they, Alida?"—she didn't pause to let Alida answer—"But it will be so worth it. This is the best way to get your foot in the door if you want to have a career in the fashion world."

This girl was gutsy. What she had said was basically neutral, but it was the way she said it that was sort of, I don't know, offensive. She was so confident. And patronizing. It was as if she owned the place.

"So, now I'll hand it over to you, Alida, but let me also introduce my friends, because they hate public speaking. This is Cecilia Barney," she said, motioning to Heidi Klum's clone, "and this is Jane St. John," she said, pointing to the brunette.

Both girls lowered their eyes and smiled slightly. "Say hello!" commanded Daphne.

Her friends mumbled something and Daphne smiled as if to say "these guys," and then they all walked to the front row and sat down.

"Okay, so let's continue," said Alida.

The rest of the meeting progressed and Alida explained protocol, rules, safety, and everything else. I listened attentively, but every once in a while my eyes were drawn to the backs of Daphne, Cecilia, and Jane. Just their posture seemed intimidating.

Finally, the meeting was wrapping up, and Alida took on a serious tone. "Lastly, I want to say that you will all be assigned to different editors by the end of the day. Once you get your editor, there can be no trading, unless the editor requests a change. But there is one position that will not be decided today, and that is

the most coveted one: assistant to Genevieve West, the editor in chief." Alida said Genevieve's name with reverence. "That will be rewarded in two weeks' time and based on performance. It is a demanding job, and only *one* of you will get it. Even though it's challenging, no one will get an education like the one they get under Genevieve's tutelage. So I suggest you all work hard at your various posts, because that is the only way you have a chance at working in the editor in chief's office."

I knew then and there that I had to have that internship with Genevieve. That would be like the apex for me. I planned to bust my butt over the next few weeks, take additional assignments, offer to help anyone, and do whatever was needed to get that job.

Daphne raised her hand and Alida nodded. "Last year Genevieve had *two* interns—why not this year?" asked Daphne petulantly.

"She thought it got a little hectic, all the people in her office," said Alida.

"She's such a nut," said Daphne with obvious fondness. "Okay, girlies," she said, rising and signaling to her friends. Then they all stood up.

Alida seemed surprised slash annoyed that Daphne had called an end to the meeting but didn't say anything and instead stood up also. "The sign-up for which editor you want to work for is over here," she said, motioning to the corner.

Daphne and her friends continued walking out of the room. "I'm working for *you* again, Alides," said Daphne with a smile.

"And put Cecilia down with Richard and Jane down with Stephanie," she said, more of a command than a request.

Alida nodded, her brow furrowed. It was obvious that Alida was not psyched for Daphne to work for her again.

As soon as Daphne and her gaggle left, everyone else seemed to exhale and ran over to the sign-up sheet. Did they have some sort of prior knowledge of who was nice and who wasn't? 'Cause I sure didn't.

"Who are you going for?" I asked Gabe.

"I put myself down for Warren Frank. He's a queen, too, and brilliant with photographers. I heard he's a bit of a diva, but I think I can handle it," said Gabe.

"What about you?" I asked Teagan.

"Slim pickings, but Viv Mercer, the sittings editor."

I glanced at the list. All that was left was CeCe Ward, the bookings editor who was supposed to be the devil, or someone named Mary-Elizabeth Fillerton, who worked in fact-checking. I didn't want to spend the entire summer stuck in some room surfing the net to find out what year Cindy Crawford and Richard Gere divorced or other boring stuff like that, so I took a deep breath and wrote my name down next to CeCe's. I prayed that rumors of her nefarious exploits were exaggerated. But it didn't matter, anyway, because I planned on working there for only two weeks before I made my move to the editor in chief's office.

When I noticed everyone had left the room, I leaned into Gabe and Teagan.

"So what was the deal with that girl Daphne? She seemed to think she, like, *owns* the place," I joked.

"Sweetie, she *does* own the place! Didn't you hear her last name?" asked Gabe.

"I don't remember."

"Hughes. As in Mortimer Hughes. As in her daddy is our boss's boss's boss, the big kahuna," said Gabe.

I took a deep breath. Ahhh, now I got it. Wow. No wonder she was so bossy. And confident. I guess billions'll do that.